Dreaded Invocations: Terrifying Horror Tales to Utter in Hushed Tones

Anthony M. Caro

Published by Anthony M. Caro, 2024.

Table of Contents

Inhumane Resources

Everyone wants a fair shot at a job, but few people like to go through a job interview, especially one with Mr. Yons. Even those who usually shine in interviews come out of sessions with Yons feeling dim.

"How long did you work for Yazzir Personal Protection Services?" Yons didn't try to hide his utter boredom when asking Bruce the question.

"Long enough to know I was there too long." Bruce thought a touch of levity would work in his favor. Nothing worked to gain favor from Yons.

"How long did you work for Fireleeves Enterprises?"

"That was a temp job for six weeks," Bruce fired back defensively but sternly. The prospective employee prepared for that question.

"Six weeks? And how long did you work for the Steamshot Corporation?"

"Three weeks through a temp agency."

"You change jobs a lot." Yons' statement had an accusatory undertone.

"True, after I left bodyguard and personal protection work, I bounced a bit." Bruce opted for the honest approach.

"How long did you work..."

Bruce had life experience, although he wouldn't call all his experiences in life positive. He had to deal with hostile and dangerous people night after night. Bruce expected such behavior in his long-ago chosen full-time profession and never took anything personally. However, he never expected someone to call him for a mundane job interview and behave so hostile and disinterested 15 seconds into the ordeal.

"I noticed on the classified ads that your company uses the Moonlighter temp agency." Bruce tried to gain control of the conversation by throwing Yon's company's HR partnerships back at him.

"How long did you work for..."

"I'm sure an HR specialist with your experience knows a temp agency provides temporary fill-in services that save companies money. Helps people between jobs, too." Bruce's offense-by-defense replies sought to gain control of the conversation.

Yons had more than a thimble of dislike for assertive Bruce.

"You have a six-month gap in your employment history."

"I also have combat zone experience, emergency medical technician experience, and performed personal protection services. I handle pressure well. Mostly"

"You have a six-month gap, suggesting unemployment from late 1980 into 1981."

"Yes, it's on the résumé I sent you. I'm sure you review all résumés before contacting an applicant you're considering." Bruce knew the score.

Yons had already decided who to hire for the job Bruce sought. Truthfully, someone high above Yons on the company ladder made the predetermined call.

That didn't mean Yons called off other interviews. He had to go through the show-trial motions to make it appear the company picked the best person from the broadest pool. Bruce understood the game but kept the show going, hoping to steer it under control. Professional tough guys don't like losing control or being played for a fool.

"Why do you have a six-month gap?"

Show-trial interviews helped create the illusion that some Exec VP's relative topped all those enthusiastic and highly qualified hat throwers. It's all about putting on a show, with the bulk of the entertainment value serving the organ grinder's amusement. Yons had much fun with each applicant's ordeal, appreciating boredom-alleviating attention and supplication from those on the other side of the desk.

The disinterested HR specialist continued. "The gap?"

"Personal circumstances."

"Tells me nothing."

"Hard to work when you're sick."

"Does work make you sick?"

"You could say some of my past jobs did. That's why I don't do that work anymore."

"I hope you've gotten better."

"Me, too."

Yons' disinterest morphed into hostility, and he opened a cigar box near the phone and stapler on his desk. No cigars inside the box. Yons didn't smoke. The box housed rubber bands, scissors, pens, and pencils. Yons took the pencil not to write notes. He took no notes from the sham interview. The pencil existed to tap the desk impatiently.

"Do you plan on getting sick again in the future?" Yons like to yank chains.

"Anyone can get sick. People get sick all the time. On birthdays. On wedding anniversaries. Graduations."

"Are they looking for a job?"

"You can get sick."

Yons started spin-tapping the pencil. Tap with the eraser, spin, tap with the tip, and repeat.

"I'm not looking for a job." Yons' comments stuck Bruce like a knife. Bruce's previous career gave him a lot of experience getting stuck with knives.

"No, you're not looking for a job. You got yours." Bruce knew a bit about knife handles.

Yons stopped spinning and tapping. Staring served as the now-preferred belligerent action.

"How did your childhood shape your professional life?" Yons thought he'd amuse himself by throwing an irrelevant curveball.

"Miserably. No worries. I am an adult now."

"Can you give me one reason why I should hire you?"

"That's an aggressive question."

The response took Yons slightly aback. "Is there a good reason why I shouldn't ask it?"

"It stokes aggression." Bruce's confrontational comment preceded professional advice. "Calm is better than aggressive. Aggressive people aren't predictable."

Yons leaned back and sunk into his chair. If his facial expression and body language told a story, tossing the pencil into the cigar box - where it bounced off the scissors before landing and spinning on the floor - gave away the ending.

"Do you have any questions for me before we conclude?" Yons sincerely had "conclude" on his mind.

"Do you run with scissors?"

Yons blinked twice, trying to register Bruce's turn at a curveball question. Did he hear the question correctly?

"Excuse me?"

"Do you run with scissors? Those scissors?" Bruce nodded his head toward the cigar box and its contents.

"You reading one of those pop psychology 'survive a job interview' books?" Yons scoffed. "If you are, you're reading bound and printed trash."

"Could you answer the question?"

"No."

"So you don't run with scissors."

"No. Meaning, I'm not answering the question."

"Have you ever been to the zoo? Do you go to the zoo?"

Yons leaned forward and put his elbow tips on the desk to support his head in his hands.

"Recently or since I was a child?"

"Either."

"Yes."

"Did you bring a stick with you?"

"A stick? What kind of stick? A walking stick?" Yons wouldn't let a hat-in-hand alpha male beggar decide how the interview ends, so he kept the show going.

"Poking. Poking stick. Did you poke a dangerous animal with a stick inside its cage?"

"No."

"Yes, you did."

"No sticks. No pokes."

Yons nervously pushed his chair away from the desk, preceding his attempt to stand.

"Does your mouth poke anything? Do you run your mouth because you think an animal plays safe in an office cage?"

"Okay, okay. You gave up. You don't think you're getting the job. Fine. You can hit the bar and brag about how you showed me up. Go ahead. Save some face. Tell everyone else in the bar who needs a job."

"You didn't run with scissors because it's dangerous, but you left scissors on the desk. That's not safe. I learned to be alert to things like that before my first day of bodyguard school."

"Okay, we know it's time to go."

Yons tried to stand up aggressively but misjudged the distance. His knees bumped into the desk, knocking him back into the chair.

"It's out of place. The scissors should be inside a desk drawer. It's safer for everyone to have sharp objects in a safe place. You never asked anything about my previous professional services. If you did, I'd tell you never do anything that makes an environment unsafe."

"It's great they're out of danger, and you need to be out of here now."

"If you'd ask me a legit question about my recent and past jobs, I'd tell you about dangerous people, dangerous situations, and all the stress they bring to the mind."

"Come on, the interview's over."

Yons pushed himself further from the desk, giving himself enough clearance to stand so he could walk to the door, which gave Bruce a big hint to walk to the door and keep going.

"Can't believe 'resource person' who deals with 'humans' never learned what dangerous and hostile environments - work and otherwise - do to the head."

The human resource pro didn't move one foot before Bruce's arm shot out, grabbing Yons by the hair.

"There's only so much someone can take spending night after night in hostile environments."

Bruce pulled Yons forward by the hair before the experienced and adept HR professional could yell, slamming him face down into the oak desk's surface—up and down, three times - banging Yons' head enough times to rattle the brain.

Bruce torqued Yons' head enough that the impact stunned all those little invisible brain wires no one could see. Bruce's past experiences educated him about messed up brain wires. Yons, however, couldn't understand why he couldn't get the words out when he wanted to scream and alert anyone still working down the hall 30 minutes past the end of the work day.

"There's only so much the head can take." Bruce continued, speaking from personal and professional experience.

Screaming would soon become harder. Bruce yanked Yons up by the hair, slipped the open cigar box underneath him, and slammed him face-first into it.

Bruce's palm pressed down, driving Yons' face painfully into the box. One hand did the job fine - Bruce drove his weight down through his arm and jammed Yons' into the box and its pencils, pens, and paperclips. Yons tried to speak, but words only came out muffled. It was hard to talk when a pencil pierced through a lip.

Moving his head proved impossible, but he realized he had no trouble darting his eyes side-to-side. Bruce situated himself to the right, and Yons instinctively looked left, maybe hoping to see someone was there to help. After a split-second of self-delusion, the eyes moved right, and he could see Bruce over the cigar box's edge.

The surprisingly clear image revealed Bruce had taken the scissors out of that obnoxious $1.99 cigar box and held them at the ready in his free hand.

Yons struggled as much as he could, but moving Bruce's arm proved impossible. Had the HR specialist read the resume, he'd know attempts to move the interviewee physically would fall short.

The interviewer had no appreciation for the powerlessness he felt, to say nothing of the humiliation. Abject terror, don't forget abject terror. Terror ran down Yons' spine when he felt Bruce starting to cut his hair with the scissors. Bruce didn't always snip.

Sometimes, he just closed the scissors around a clump of hair and ripped it out.

"You know what's worse than a six-month gap in employment history?"

More haircutting. More hair pulling. Lots of bleeding. Soon, less hair. So much bleeding. Many muffled cries.

"Six months of consistent employment complete with six months of unofficial warnings. Repeated warnings. Repeated warnings from supervisors telling someone whose job involves basic security at a residence for very sick people - people who are sick in the head from stress. Sick in the head and dangerous and extremely dangerous to themselves and others. That's why you got to follow protocol - keep doors and windows locked. Otherwise, the sick-in-the-head patients get ideas when they pass windows. But an incompetent worker who doesn't understand safety won't do their job right."

Bruce soon grew bored with cutting and ripping out hair.

"That's consistency in the workforce. Incompetent consistency. No resume gaps, though."

Bruce showed initiative by moving beyond a malicious haircut and putting the scissors to work on flesh and skull.

"But who's going to fire the guy in charge of the psycho wing's relative?"

Envy's an Art Form

E nvy is the worst of the seven deadly sins. At least somebody can enjoy themself with the other six, including sloth.

Harry's envy of that awful painting hanging in the corporate office's reception area proved a theory about the seven deadly sins: they lead to more sins. The ripple effect brought Harry to the building's entrance. At three in the morning, he stood soldier-like at the front door, holding a delivery bag containing food he paid for, a mock combination platter intended for a phony delivery.

Envy makes people think and do dumb things.

Not that Harry felt inclined to call his plan anything other than brilliant. He had an artist's mind and came up with a crazy strategy to rid the world - and the office building's reception area - of that wretched painting.

Harry waved at the security guard on the other side of the front door's thick glass, and the guard buzzed him inside. You'd think the guard would feel alarmed about someone wearing a wind scarf and a plastic helmet that hid their features. It wasn't unusual for delivery pros to don accessories to protect their face from the wind and cold while riding around. Delivery folks, like artists, were an odd lot. They had no issues traveling aimlessly by bike in freezing weather at 3 AM for a few dollars.

Artists and food delivery pros shared traits because, well, lots of artists had to deliver food to make a living, at least until someone discovered their more creative work.

Enough food-delivering artists were bicycling around 24/7 to lull the front desk security guard's suspicions. People work late and order food late. He buzzed Harry inside.

Harry had only been inside for 30 seconds before the security guard turned lawgiver.

"You can't go to the upper floors." The guard pointed out the rule after Harry told him he needed to drop the food off at the doorstep on the 22nd floor.

The security guard picked up the desk phone to call the room and advise the occupant that their food had arrived.

"Hold on! Instructions say no calls, door knocking, bell ringing, or disturbances." Harry held up his smartphone but ensured the security guard couldn't see the screen.

The guard stared for a second. His face had that "Why are you making my job hard?" look preceding the words, "You aren't going up there."

"Am I saying I want to take an elevator ride?" Harry retorted. "How about we do this? Could you drop the food off upstairs for me and take a photo?"

"Take a photo?"

"Yeah, and I'll take a picture of the picture. I need proof of the drop-off."

The security guard shrugged, probably realizing that the trip up the elevator would break up his dull evening routine. Besides, what could Harry do? Without an elevator code, he couldn't go exploring.

"There's nothing in the reception area worth stealing," the security guard thought as the elevator doors closed. "He can hang for a bit and look at all the pretty paintings on the walls."

The guard took the food to office #2213 on the 22nd floor.

Once those elevator doors closed, Harry fixated his eyes on that miserable, rotten painting hanging on the wall. Oh, all the paintings hanging on the wall were rotten and miserable, per Harry.

The goofy, abstract/surreal/neomodern/junk *la Peinture* that his old hated art class colleague Cosmo painted ranked highest on all things rotten and miserable. (Also, per Harry.)

Harry wouldn't accept that Cosmo beat Harry's nouveau cool painting in the building management's publicity-generating local art contest.

Harry had delivered food to this office before. Besides knowing the room numbers, he had an idea how much time he had before the security guard would return.

The scheming artist went into business quickly. He pulled the disparaging painting off the wall without worrying about security cameras catching him. Harry had the helmet and face scarf, a de facto supervillain costume, to hide his identity.

Nobody would recognize Harry's appearance as if they didn't acknowledge his artistic brilliance. The property management's decision to pick Cosmo's painting over Harry's was the last obscurity-supporting slight the self-proclaimed creative genius accepted.

Harry wouldn't settle for second best, and he wouldn't be second best if something happened to that first-place vulgarity.

Time to put all that envy and anger to good use.

Harry yanked the painting from the wall and looked at it briefly to ensure he had Cosmo's artwork. It took one second to bring forth an envious rage, leading him to smash the framed artwork on the front desk's hard surface. Glass flew everywhere when Harry freed the painting from its confines.

Harry despised Cosmo like he despised all other so-called artists and no-talents topping him on sales and good words. The faux delivery person felt glee as he ripped and tore the painting to shreds before crumpling the shreds into canvas balls.

What's another deadly sin that's pretty good? *Wrath.* Harry enjoyed feeling wrath after ripping up that fatuous brush, paint, and palette-born monstrosity.

"Rig a contest and cheat me?" Harry deluded himself as he continued to tear the painting.

Okay, envious wrath concluded—time to go. Shame the door won't open.

Guess those automatic doors only open automatically during the day when daytime only necessitates engaging the electronic lock behind the security desk for entries and not exits.

Pushing on the door didn't open it, no matter how much wrath fired up Harry's pushes.

"What the hell happened to that frame?" Yelled the now-returning security guard upon exiting the elevator and looking at broken plastic and glass on the floor.

Harry turned and replied, "It fell."

"How the hell did the painting get ripped up and crumpled?"

"It fell, too."

The security guard made a beeline towards the desk and the EMERGENCY button near the phone.

Harry knew things would get worse when the cops came. Shame his temperament never allowed him to figure out how to keep worse from becoming more worse than worse.

Tackling a security guard worsens what's worse - especially when a guard hits his cranium on the desk's corner, splits his head open, and suffers a fractured skull. Appropriately, his weak-handed last action in life involved hitting the emergency button.

Time to go through the door fast, which isn't easy without the necessary code.

Numerical codes. All the buttons on the desk allowed a knowledgeable person to type the numerical codes and be able to open the door. Harry knew he'd never guess the code in one hundred years, much less by the time the cops came. So, Harry did the next worst thing. He grabbed the desk's chair and started smashing at the glass door - setting off a loud alarm.

If the cops weren't in a rush before, they're in a rush now.

Harry kept smashing at the glass door frantically, hoping to make a big enough hole to leap through. The chair worked okay as a blunt instrument but didn't perform a thorough job. Harry started kicking the glass door, fueled by deadly sin adrenaline. Nervousness led him to make a wider opening by grabbing and pulling shards and chunks of glass out with his bare hands. He ignored the severe cuts they made.

The police would soon arrive, so Harry forced himself through the makeshift and narrow portal, not caring about the shards of glass cutting him here and there from top to bottom. Beloved adrenaline might dull pain and fuel a fool to pedal wildly down the street on a bicycle into the night. For about one hundred feet, it may.

At about one-hundred-and-three feet, poor Harry fell off his bike and collapsed.

⎯⎯⎯◉⎯⎯⎯

THE SUN ROSE AT DAWN, casting light on the empty city streets. Rush hour wouldn't arrive for another 63 minutes, meaning the police needed to move quickly to get Harry's corpse off the sidewalk, onto the coroner's van, and on its way to the morgue.

Two officers in blue looked down on Harry's body. A massive pool of blood formed between

Harry's face-down body and the pavement. No surprises why. Anyone looking at the crime scene photographs would see the small, medium, and large cuts - shallow and not-so-shallow lacerations - made by the glass shards.

The glass shards had a little help from Harry's lack of care or brains in rushing through a tight gauntlet of broken glass.

Blood didn't only collect in a pool at the street corner. The crimson fluid was everywhere, spraying onto store windows and car hoods. That's what happens when you sever an artery. Or two.

One cop looked down the street at the long trails of blood that led from the broken glass door to Harry's almost final resting place.

Both cops directed their eyes down at Harry with quizzical looks.

"What do you think this guy was up to?"

"Don't know. Maybe he wanted to paint the town red."

Looking Up from the Trenches

Your eyes open. Your eyes can open because your eyelids are light enough for what little strength you have left. Your limbs won't move. Despite all your best efforts, they can't or won't move. They feel chained to the ground and secured by heavy weights. You worry about whether a Gotha G.V. dropped a bomb that rendered you armless and legless, as they did to so many "basket cases" serving in the ongoing Great War.

Is it still ongoing?

You feel like you've been asleep for weeks. Who's to say you haven't?

If there were any Gotha G.V. planes in the skies above, you didn't see them. Since you can't move your head, all you can see is the Belgian sky. The once beautiful blue sky appears oddly indistinct, displaying a mix of the falling sun and the yellow-brown chemical haze of mustard gas.

That god-awful gas lingers everywhere on the Western Front. Your facemask offers some protection, but the gas has a way of seeping inside. After bleeding into the mask, the gas finds its way to the lungs, burning the respiratory tract to uselessness.

Mustard gas also burns the eyes, and you know you aren't blind since you can see the sky, as ugly as it appears today. (Tonight?)

You laugh to yourself, appreciating the one good stroke of luck you experienced since arriving on the Western Front - you collapsed onto your back and not facedown in the muddy trenches. Lying face down in the mud would mean you'd only see the dirt.

Then you might think you were blind. Maybe you are blind, and the hazy sky is nothing more than your mind playing games to keep you sane.

What of those Gotha G.V. warplanes? You'd hear them if they were out of your line of vision. Maybe you're blind and deaf. Did the Great War take your sense of smell away? You don't pick up the scent - the obtuse garlic scent - of mustard gas drifting over and into the Western Front's trenches.

You know there's mustard gas here.

You saw the yellow-brown clouds drifting across the trenches, swallowing so many of your fellow soldiers.

Where are your fellow soldiers?

Since you can't move your head and your eyes only dart so far, you don't know if they fell to the ground beside you. You don't hear them, either. Of course, you wouldn't see or hear the dead moving.

You can smell mustard gas. Why can't you smell the troops?

Where did the ever-omnipresent smell of now-decaying flesh go?

You lack the strength to move your body, so you will yourself to at least get a better look at your surroundings.

Lift, lift, lift your head.

You find the strength to lift the back of your skull and pull free of the mud as you finally raise your head, with your chin tucked into your prone chest.

You see your body from the lower chest down. Intact. No bomb blew it apart. You never felt more appreciative of the muddy, filthy combat fatigues before now.

You don't know when you first started hearing the crunching sounds drifting in the air, but you hear them now. The joy of regaining your hearing gives you enough strength to shake the paralysis, at least some of it. You can slightly raise your shoulders from the ground and see more than your body lying flat. You see boots.

Soldiers' boots.

The boots make crunching sounds when they stomp through the hardening mud, marching onward.

Where they march, you don't know. You try to open your mouth, but your lips barely move. You want to call out to them, but you can't. You want to grab them with your arm, but you can't.

You can move your fingers. No, it's not a mere involuntary muscle reflex action. You prove that by opening and closing your hand into a fist.

You start banging your fist, *both fists,* into the ground by snapping your hands at the wrist. Can they hear the sounds?

Don't despair. If you can move anything slightly, you can move everything slightly. If you can move anything, you can move everything.

Get up.

Is willpower enough to let you sit up?

Yes.

The effort is Herculean, but you manage to sit up. You look around. You're still on the battlefield, lying near the trenches. So many dead bodies lay around you. The living soldiers walk, and they walk right into a massive cloud of fog.

Brown and yellow fog.

Not fog. Mustard gas.

You open your mouth to yell, but you cannot. You want to touch your comrades, but you cannot. You want to stand up.

You can stand up.

You want to run, but you cannot. Still, you can walk. You want to save your comrades.

Can you?

Yes. So Walk.

Your legs feel brutally heavy. The mud underneath makes walking harder, but you chase after your fellow soldiers. You want to warn them to stay away from the mustard gas cloud.

The last soldier in the formation line is the only soldier who has not yet walked through the mustard gas cloud. You walk faster.

Faster.

You almost catch him as he nears that brownish-yellowish cloud.

Save him.

Your hand reaches for the gas mask straps under his helmet and at the base of his neck. Your fingers wrap around the straps, and you use the straps as a leash to pull the soldier back, but the gas mask and helmet come off.

The soldier keeps walking. You look at the gas mask in your hand and the helmet that falls to the ground. You look back at the soldier.

He has no head, but he walks. He walks right into the yellow-brown cloud.

Where are you?

You turn around to look at where you once laid still.

And you still lay unmoving.

Your body rests quietly on the battlefield by a trench. It's not alone — so many bodies.

Scared, you want to run away, and you do.

You run into the cloud. It's no longer a garish yellow-brown cloud. Once you enter, the colors turn to white, and a white cloud is all you see.

You keep walking and walking and walking. For how long, you don't know.

You stop when you see the stairs. You look up and see the stairs go on to infinity.

Not to infinity - The stairs go to white clouds, beautiful white clouds in the sky.

You start your ascent up the stairs.

You never understood why you fought in the Great War, but whatever the reason, it was worth the effort.

Inhale in Hell

"My man, I ain't feeling it." Jimmy held the pipe in his hand. Small amounts of smoke smoldered from the contraband Jimmy lit. The cloud of rough-stuff smoke Jimmy exhaled impressed.

"Draw it in," Sammy advised, backing away from his customer. Sammy backed away, not out of fear but because he didn't want to inhale an iota of that cloud. He wouldn't touch that junk for a million bucks. Sell it for $75? Deal.

Jimmy brought his lighter to the pipe and took another deep drag. Deep inhale. Nothing.

"Still ain't feeling nothing, brother." Jimmy's words carried a hint of annoyance.

"You've gotta draw it in all the way," Sammy suggested, still backing away. "Inhale. Deep." Sammy slipped as he backed further away, almost losing his footing thanks to the garbage on the ground around the tent city. Funny that there are lots of tents but no down-on-their-luck tent tenants. All we had was Jimmy and Sammy.

Jimmy sucked in more of whatever was inside the pipe and held the smoke deep in his lungs. Man, Jimmy knew how to inhale his dope.

Inhale the dope Jimmy did. He made embarrassing slobbering sounds as he sucked on the end of the pipe. After sucking as much smoke as the human body and messed-up lungs could handle, Jimmy counted to three inside his head. He paused and looked at the pipe for a second as smoke started coming out of his nose. Jimmy figured he needed to hold in the smoke as long as possible to get that big enthusiastic high.

Nothing.

Jimmy stared at the pipe in his hand for a few seconds, waiting for something that remained nothing. He didn't move, but his eyes darted in Sammy's direction.

Sammy bragged he had a connection to the stuff with the rep for blowing minds. Smoke enough, and it'd take more than your mind. Eternal soul? Gone, daddy. Pipers dig the stuff, but only when sellers deliver on promises. Sammy made promises, but delivering? Nolo contendere.

Jimmy's staring at Sammy started to get a little - what's an educated word - malicious?

"I'm telling you, man, that stuff'll eat you up." Sammy tried to defuse a touch of Jimmy's annoyance. "Nothing out there matches it."

"No, nothing out there is this worthless."

Sammy started feeling a little nervous because he knew Jimmy would bash the dealer's skull into the pavement if he suspected a big rip-off. Jimmy had an addiction to feed, and word about the new designer mess burning up the faraway sections of the town said it made crack and meth look like $2.49 energy drinks.

Jimmy wanted that wicked, uplifting high, but that doesn't mean he was a down-and-out piper. He inherited enough money to delay down and out for at least a couple of years, even with all the daily junk he smoked, swallowed, and shot.

The man might even get some of his fortune back if he sold the pipes he kept. Not like some doper didn't have a use for them.

Sammy heard brand-new junk found its way into some "lucky" pipes floating around town. Supply stayed low, but demand grew huge. Jimmy thought Vice or some other department would spread the news about what's in the junk to scare people. They couldn't. Nobody knew its secret recipe. All people knew was that smoking that stuff gave pipe freakazoids the craziest euphoric high they would ever get.

If they could get it.

Some unlucky pipe smokers got conned. Desperate dealer schemers will pull that stunt.

Once the real-deal stuff turned up for sale, it sold out. Quick. Jimmy heard rumors that Sammy always had a hook-up, so the man and some of his inheritance headed down to a less stylish section of the city—no fear on Jimmy's part. Addictions weren't the only things that led him to toss off caution. Jimmy's willingness to beat up anybody who gave him trouble helped his wanderlust. If he couldn't curb-stomp them, he'd stab them—Jimmy's flexible.

Jimmy's also impatient. Sammy wanted the junk inside that pipe to work more than Jimmy. Crazy that straight-headed Jimmy could be worse to contend with than freaked-out, euphoric Jimmy. Euphoric Jimmy wouldn't be in a bad mood.

Sammy looked at the empty, desolate tent city to see if anyone was around. Why bother? Nobody in the ghost town would come running to help him if that junk-and-pipe combo platter didn't work some magic.

Soon.

Jimmy second-guessed all vouchers for dope-dealing Sammy's character and his rep for delivering. Did Sammy plan on pulling a fast one with Jimmy? That'd be a bad plan. Con jobbers quickly found themselves in a mess when giving Jimmy a hard time. Sammy should have known the score.

"You joking with me?" Jimmy blurted words that caught Sammy by surprise. "Is this all a joke?"

Words swerved into accusations.

"Come on, my man," Sammy tried pawning off Jimmy's concerns. "Why would I play funny stuff?"

Jimmy hated wasting time, and he wasted time on junk that wasn't getting him high. Whatever Sammy put in a pipe had no relation to the crazy euphoric stuff everybody's raving about. Or was Sammy conned by his supplier? Jimmy didn't know.

Jimmy couldn't see how Sammy intended to rip him off. The five or six puffs Jimmy took from the pipe were all freebies. Sammy didn't take any money from him. The dealer gave his prospects free sample inhales. If Jimmy felt a hundred percent that Sammy was playing some angle, he'd be pounding on the dealer's skull.

The whole free puff game made Jimmy wonder a little about the scheme, but only a little. Jimmy didn't ask for or want any free samples. He expected to pay a premium for a small amount, which is why he had cash in both pockets.

Jimmy finally remembered he had cash in his pockets. He also had a conclusion in his head.

"Your party guests running late?" Jimmy asked with an ill-reputable tone.

"What?" Sammy snapped out of daydreaming when Jimmy's last puff of rank smoke hit him in the face. He didn't hear Jimmy's angry words too clearly, at least not the first time around.

"Is everybody late for the party?" Jimmy yelled. "You're planning a surprise party for me, aren't you?"

"Hold on, man! Keep it down! Keep it down! The place doesn't look like much, but this is a quiet neighborhood here." Sammy held his hands in an "I don't know/I give up" gesture.

"You trying to surprise me? Is that what all this melodrama is about?" Jimmy jammed the pipe into Sammy's shirt pocket.

"Melodrama?" Sammy didn't get the meaning. He backed away a bit while slipping a hand into his shirt pocket. He didn't want the pipe on his person for one second.

"The melodrama that is soon to come, huh?" Jimmy's voice turned threatening as he placed his hand on Sammy's shirt pocket, jamming Sammy's hand and the pipe in place.

"Melodrama. Action. Thrills." Jimmy's cryptic words left Sammy confused. So, Jimmy filled him in, "All the action, chills, and thrills that were supposed to happen when your guys showed up, except they aren't showing up."

Sammy began to see Jimmy's meaning.

"Jimmy, man, maybe that stuff's working in mysterious ways. Your head's not thinking right about me." Sammy tried moving back further, but Jimmy's hand made a fist, grabbing ahold of the shirt pocket, the shirt, and, by default, Sammy.

"You guys wanted to roll me, right?" Jimmy yanked Sammy's shirt hard while Sammy shook his head, suggesting, "No." Jimmy pressed. "You stall, and your pals jump me from behind, and all three of you run off with my money, right?"

"Come on, Jimmy," Sammy pleaded. "I ain't about that."

"Looks like your pals never showed, and it also looks like I'm gonna preempt your melodrama with a night of championship boxing." Jimmy pulled his fist back to set up an intended one-shot knockout until he felt a sharp pain in his gut, stunning him.

Jimmy wanted to take a shot at Sammy, but a second sharp pain loosened his fingers and grip. The tough guy let go of the dealer's shirt and doubled over on the sidewalk in front of a tent.

"I don't feel so good." Those were the only words coming out of Jimmy's mouth. Hard for him to talk with rotgut stuff rising in the back of his throat.

"Sorry, Jimmy, you don't know the score." Sammy walked a little closer to the doubled-over Jimmy. Jimmy looked up from the sidewalk position with disgust for the crooked dealer.

"The stuff people been smoking. It's experimental voodoo." Sammy kept going with the bad news. "It does crazy things to the mind. Rots it."

Jimmy's eyes bugged.

"No, man. Don't worry about what you smoked," Sammy said. "The crazy stuff wasn't in the pipe."

After Jimmy registered Sammy's words, worry went away, leaving his anger on its lonesome. Jimmy tried to stand up to give Sammy the shot in the face he deserved, but Jimmy fell back to the ground before getting off his knees. Jimmy puked the rising rotgut bile over the not-pristine sidewalk.

"Sorry, man. I had to make you ill. I put some bad stuff in there." Jimmy pegged Sammy for running a ruse but did it too late. He also figured out the wrong ruse. "People get hooked on the quality stuff. Hard. All they want is two things. More dope, no surprise. The other thing's crazier."

Spasms rocked Jimmy's stomach and spread to the rest of his body. He spasmed on the sidewalk, flopping like a fish.

"Jimmy, sorry, but you'd never be a regular. You'd drop me once you found an upper-scale supplier. I have to take care of my regular customers. They're the crew feeding me."

A zipper went down on a nearby tent, and a filthy arm covered in boils reached out for Jimmy's leg. The hand grabbed his foot. Another arm reached out from the tent and grabbed Jimmy's other foot. Jimmy looked up at Sammy, not still fully clued in on the angle.

"I got to help my customers feed their fix. That junk hooks you bad. And like I said, it comes with rotten mojo side effects."

The arms dragged Jimmy into the tent. He looked at Sammy with his mouth agape, unable to talk after the slow-working rank junk made him sick.

"That stuff. Rots the mind, turns you into a super freak." Sammy took a short pause before finishing. "Stimulates the appetite like a weed, only way more big time."

Jimmy's fingernails clawed into the sidewalk as his arms were the last to drag into the tent. Two sounds replaced the quiet that fell on the tent city. The tent's zipper made its sounds when zipped up, and a screaming ruckus came inside it. When the commotion died down, Sammy turned his back on the tent. The sounds coming out were quieter but not hard to peg.

Sammy knew those sounds and listened to them echo on the desolate street.

Ripping, tearing, twisting, chomping, and chewing. Give the shenanigans enough time, and the sounds of gnawing and sucking on bone would echo.

"Jimmy," Sammy spoke, not knowing if Jimmy could hear. If Jimmy could hear Sammy, he'd get good advice, "Stay away from that stuff. It'll eat you alive."

Torturous Extremus

"**I**t's not so bad, lad," said the filthy, dirty old fellow with the long beard who hung shackled to a wall from chains around his wrists. He spoke to a somewhat filthy, dirty young man sporting a half-a-day's beard growth. The unkempt younger fellow also found himself hanging by his wrists from chains and shackles affixed to the slimy dungeon wall.

The younger fellow tried not to look at the ground. He heard the vermin moving about and felt the only good thing about hanging from a wall in a dark dungeon was that nothing would chew his feet off.

His ears were another matter, not that anything would chew them off, but the clown hanging next to him seemed intent on *talking* them off.

The hanging lad didn't use the word "clown" as an insult. He saw the green, purple, and yellow stripes and patterns underneath the filth covering the old fellow. Seems court jester served as his previous occupation. As with so many other kingdom clowns, they amuse the king and others of royalty until they don't. One bad joke, and to the dungeons you go.

"I tell you, son, there can be far worse things than hanging from this wall. Terrible tortures. Some are so awful they're hard to describe. Beyond horrible. Oh, the rack. Oh, the hanging cage. Oh, the brazen bull. Oh, the chair of torture."

Oh, shut up. The hanging lad thought to himself. The hanging jester hadn't shut up for what seemed like days.

"All you can hope for is a torturer who takes pride in his work. As bad as some tortures are, they can be worse when someone knows not how to perform their duties." The hanging jester seemed oblivious that the hanging lad paid little or no attention to him.

The hanging lad didn't tell the hanging jester to keep quiet, not out of respect, but a shattered jaw makes speaking a trifle hard.

Anger swelled inside the hanging lad. Projection, it was. The hanging lad ran his mouth all over the kingdom, telling the peasants how the royalty did them wrong.

Talking about the wrong we've done you? Let's give you another wrong to talk about, they said.

Oh, the irony, telling him to talk after they smashed his jaw. They weren't done with him, either - off to the dungeon to await more tortures.

The hanging lad watched a single ray of sunlight from a single window illuminate a circle.

"My father was a jester. My grandfather was a jester. My great-grandfather started as a jester, but they moved him to the kitchen. That's what happens when you're not funny. Could cook, though. He served up much better than the once-a-day gruel they give us."

The circle grew smaller as the sun faded. When the circle disappeared, there was nothing to see inside the dungeon. Our hanging lad only wished there was nothing to hear.

"Some jesters never change up their material."

The hanging lad used his little strength to pull at his chains. Break free from the chains and shackles? An absurd thought!

"Now, a jester who mixes laughs and dancing, that's someone who..."

The hanging lad made a slight tug on the chain.

Worth the try.

"...if the funny stuff doesn't get any laughs, you can break out in a dance. Singing helps, too."

The circle of light grew large and small as the days passed in the kingdom.

It's been weeks. Is whoever's running the rack or that drawing-and-quartering thing that busy?

More days passed.

"Doing it over again, I'd make more fun of the cook and less of the king."

Is anyone coming to take me to the torture room?

"...but then you have to worry about him spitting in your food."

I'll appreciate any attention from a torturer. I wouldn't even mind the hot poker thing.

The sun rose and later set. Repeat.

Good Lord, are they going to leave me in here with a hanging jester who won't shut up?

The hanging lad looked at the locked wooden door and the sunlight shining on it. He watched the light fade, return, fade, return, fade, and return, one day to the next. Oh, the poor hanging lad's ears.

"Let me tell you about when I was young. Jesters could tell a joke without being dirty."

They are.

"They take forever to get to the funny stuff. No one cares about long setups. Get right to it."

Please let him die before me. Or let me die before him.

Both work.

Cratos the Construct and the Mysterious Cave Dweller

They called him a spawn of the Frankenstein Monster. What relation did he bear to the literary figure? None. Those who called him by the creature's name did so half out of fear and half intending to lob superiority-boosting insults.

True, Cratos the Construct shared more than a few similarities to Shelley's creation. Not long ago, they stitched body parts together where possible, only to find recently deceased pieces of organic flesh might reject one another - not a concerning problem for wayward science. Metal and robotic parts placed at appropriate points brought forth helpful non-organic assistance.

Science and steam, like dead flesh and scrap metal, have limits. So, zombie voodoo rituals quietly stepped in to further the cause.

What proportion of the Construct's life relied on modern surgery, strides in primitive robotics, and voodoo even Cratos did not know. Still, he understood people perceived him as a monster and not a scientific miracle.

Although people called him a monster and hunted him, the Construct knew he was not a monster. No friend of humanity he was, but that was humanity's choice.

Not a monster, robot, or entirely human, but a stowaway? Yes.

Cratos the Construct allowed his sharp, to-be-invented-in-the-next-century-adding machine-like mind to drift back to the night before. The being tried not to move, hiding his 7-foot frame as best he could in the rear of the horse-drawn carriage. The Construct curled in the corner by the carriage's exit, knowing he'd have to leap out before dawn after the carriage traveled far away from the uninviting village. Two horses moved the carriage mercifully, making Cratos' added weight unnoticeable.

The carriage contained hundreds of pounds of "this and that" intended for sale at saloons and hotels in the next town. The Construct could carry food and wine upon departing the trailer. At least he'd have enough for three days of wandering and hiding in the wilderness, moving through the night, looking for a safe reprieve from any humans hunting him.

The Construct's mind drifted to the previous evening. His thoughts were amazingly lucid despite severe hunger pangs stabbing at the parts made of flesh.

He remembered standing outside the cabin at the village's edge — a cabin occupied by a father and daughter.

Enhanced eyes and ears allowed Cratos to learn all he needed to know about their plight. He knew their plight by looking at the cabin's aged and worn condition.

Cratos the Construct could have stolen what little food the older man and his young daughter had at their small hovel. As much as the Construct wished not to admit, he could also be a thief. Cratos looked in the window, realized they had little for themselves, and felt that a few more days of hunger was endurable.

A loud cracking and snapping sound broke Cratos out of the daydream that slowly drifted toward a sleeping dream. The massive creature/tin man slid sideways when the carriage floor became uneven. Shelves of bounty for sale landed on top of him, but it only took seconds to get those things off his barrel chest. The Construct required additional seconds to jump from the carriage and avoid discovery. Seconds he never had.

Cratos' metal and hydraulic knee joints powered his jump from the carriage. Outside, he learned it suffered a broken wheel and realized he'd been discovered.

"Mr. Dawson! Mr. Dawson!" He found us! Come with the gun!"

A young man riding in the front of the carriage had already dismounted with a lantern in hand, choosing to investigate the wheel without delay. Or, likely, Mr. Dawson told him to do so.

"The creature that haunts the woods! He's come back!"

Cratos did not turn and run - two things the analytical and mechanical side of his mind suggested. The human element preferred to plead his case. Foolish.

"Calm down! Probably a bear!" Mr. Dawson shouted upon nearing the carriage's rear side, nonchalantly unworried about wild, hungry bears, much less mysterious legends haunting the woods. Whether a bear, a mysterious creature of the woods, or a never-before-seen Construct, Dawson had a double-barreled shotgun ready.

Cratos stood still. Dawson looked at him and muttered, "Lord above."

The Construct chose not to move, preferring to be a target. Dim lantern light offered little illumination, and Cratos would have a better chance than Dawson's errand boy if the carriage driver pulled the trigger in the dark.

"The stories! All true!" Dawson spoke more to himself than his terrified subordinate.

An explosive boom followed by a fiery muzzle flash indicated the carriage driver pulled the trigger on one shotgun barrel. A slug capable of taking down a bear only knocked Cratos off the side of the road and about six feet back. The Construct stumbled but remained standing. He felt little pain and less worry since a shotgun slug couldn't kill him but hurt in other ways.

The second slug knocked Cratos further backward, and the impact of two consecutive slugs left the man-made man's head spinning. The shock to the system had an effect, and Cratos nearly lost consciousness while standing. The confusion gave the carriage driver a chance to reload two more shotgun shells into his long gun.

Cratos wasted time attempting to appeal to reason. One sight of the misshapen living dead clockwork creature evoked the same reaction among all the crowds: unwarranted violence.

The third shotgun slug hurt in the traditional painful way.

Although blasted even further back, Cratos sensed something. *Senses.* A sense of smell picked up on salt, and an enhanced ear heard waves crashing. He was near the ocean, but how far?

Backing up further, the Construct received an answer. His heels ran out of the ground, and the robot creature stood at the edge of a cliff, the sea likely below.

The fourth shotgun slug arrived as expected, sending Cratos off the cliff.

Time froze as the robot monster fell into the darkness below, expecting to land in the sea. Perhaps the slugs jarred his mind so much he did not put facts together. The waves crashed on a beach, and so did Cratos the Construct.

Mercifully, he landed on the sand and not the adjacent jetty of jagged rocks.

Cratos looked up and saw the two men, the lantern illuminating them. The cliff's edge stood higher than Cratos realized. Maybe that's why he couldn't move. The fall took far more out of his seemingly indestructible frame. *Seemingly.*

The drop stunned Cratos, leaving him feeling dead, even as the continually pumping breathing machine in his chest kept him alive.

Cratos' eyes drifted up towards the cliff's topside. One natural eye and one crude, telescope-inspired orb tried their best but could see nothing in the darkness. Sharp ears heard words over the crashing waves.

"Come away from here. They can't see you in the darkness, but take no chances."

Cratos barely made out the speaker's form in the moonlight. Diminutive she was.

"Move and hide. Once the sun rises, they'll come looking for you."

II.

Come looking, they did.

"He's gone." The old crone muttered the words contemptuously to the Sheriff, his two fellow deputies, and the horses they rode in on.

"So why don't I see any footprints?" The Sheriff wondered accusingly, not even looking at the sandy beach. Eyes focused on the old crone, waiting for a reaction. None came. "Nothing you wish to say?" The Sheriff levied another accusation without accusing. "Nothing at all to say, Maria?"

At least now the old crone had a name. And a response.

"Because the big oaf couldn't stand. He fell off a damn 40-foot cliff."

The Sheriff's horse turned its head toward the deputies, both aimless on horseback. The Sheriff yanked at the reins, pulling the horse's head in Maria's direction.

"A fall any worse than four shotgun slugs to the chest? Handled them well."

"You mean well enough." Maria turned her head, barely able to hide her dismissive laughter.

The Sheriff merely stared at Maria, and she sighed before saying, "I can't show you a footprint, but here, what do your eyes think of all those fine handprints?

The Sheriff failed to deliver a comeback, for he had none. Maria, the old crone who lived by the sea, continued.

"Here's part of a footprint for you. Over there's where he dragged his legs and feet. The poor fellow went crawling to the sea to swim away. Probably drowned."

"Why risk drowning? Who'd crawl with broken legs and a broken back into the sea?" A reasonable investigative question from the lawman.

"Could be somebody shot him four times for no reason, and he felt scared."

"How do you know they had no reason?" The Sheriff asked a pointed question.

"If he were as awful as they say, he'd have snapped their necks."

The Sheriff ignored the comment and kicked the horse lightly. The animal and lawman trotted toward the old crone's beaten-up little hut underneath a cliff.

"Where's the cave? And the rock? I want to see them." The Sheriff pulled the reins to the left, moving the horse's head. The Sheriff already knew where to go.

"Oh, you don't think..." Maria feigned a fake laugh.

The horse stopped. The Sheriff looked over his shoulder at Maria.

"I think you have a bit too much of an interest in the stranger. Maybe he's not much of a stranger."

The old woman barely had the strength to lift her finger, as tired as she was. Maria managed to waste energy pointing to the destination the Sheriff already knew.

"Over there. Cave and rock. Where they've been for 20 years."

The Sheriff glanced at the massive boulder that blocked the cave's mouth. The boulder covered almost the entirety of the cave's entrance.

"Entirety" meant the boulder sealed everything except a fairly small hole at the righthand corner. The makeshift crawlspace provided enough room for a grown person to stick their hand or head into the cave. Someone small in stature and mental capacity might even crawl inside.

The Sheriff got down on his knees, having no intention to reach, peer, and certainly not crawl into the darkness. He tried to look through the hole, a challenging task since he kept his head a good five feet away.

"I don't see anything in the darkness," the Sheriff continued, "I hear something. Something moving."

Maria, the old crone, said nothing. Instincts spoke silently, saying, "Keep your mouth shut." To herself, she smiled faintly when the Sheriff made a sour face.

"Damn. I can smell him."

The Sheriff got back onto his feet, being sure to walk backward, not wanting his feet too close to that tiny hole.

"Will a description of the smell enter your official report?"

The Sheriff matched the snide comment with an exceptionally dirty look. He had no love for Maria, and she mutually disdained him.

"Something's not right. I know it's not right." The Sheriff continued his thinking aloud with a probing question, "What are the chances there are two...things...running around?"

"Ask God."

"You believe God made those things?"

"You don't think so?"

"No."

"If it was not God who made them, it was the devil, but why would the devil stop at two?"

The Sheriff looked beyond the hut's door, thinking for a second.

Maria cut off his thoughts with another question: "What would you expect to find in my hut? Does it look like I have enough room for ma' self, much less a wayward giant?"

"I like to be thorough." The Sheriff's lack of trust hung in his words.

"Thorough?" Maria rolled the word with derision. "So you want to be thorough? Then why not come tonight and give the stars above a thorough reading? Why don't you tell me what they say?"

The Sheriff and his horse ceased moving in the hut's direction.

Maria had more to say. "You keep pressing me, and you can read the stars above all by yourself from this day onward!"

III.

Except for the massive pile of blankets on top of a spare bed, the hut's interior appeared more orderly and clean than a visitor would think.

Maria started yanking off the blankets, one after the other, taking weight off the bedframe below them. The wooden bedframe carried ample weight, yet the small-in-stature Maria managed to move it away. Upon clearing the bedframe, Maria began pulling up floorboards that weren't nailed down. While most would expect sand underneath the floorboards, the section underneath the easily removable floorboard revealed what looked like a hidden grave lined by lumber walls.

The grave seemed exceptionally huge, deep and wide enough to hide a giant. And hide a giant it did. Now, nothing hid a nearly 7-foot-tall guest.

Cratos looked up from his hiding place, not knowing what to expect.

"They're gone, friend. But expect them to come back."

Cratos' eyes gave no tells about how he felt. The Construct turned his head to the small windows in the hut. Darkness revealed that the sun had long set. Maria made sure Cratos remained inside the underground hideaway during the day until well into the night. No interlopers would come at night.

"Before they return, we should talk."

◦

CRATOS SAT ON THE FLOOR of the small hut. Sitting lacked comfort. Standing risked hitting his head on the ceiling, and the Construct intended not to offend his host nor make himself look the fool. Cratos understood he "looked like a monster" but also knew behavior often shaped impressions.

Anyone attempting to describe Cratos would struggle to make sense of a patchwork creature. The body parts came from many different corpses, creating an asymmetrical look - arms and legs didn't match size-wise relative to the torso.

Did they mix and match corpses with grandfather clocks? Cratos' metal components, well, *clashed* with the organic ones.

The old crone looked like an old crone. When she spoke, she revealed a cunning nature complementing her world-weary looks.

"I see stitches where the human parts meet. Wouldn't expect such embroidery to hold together if you landed on the rocks." Maria told her guest. "Hit the sand, you did. Missed the rocks by a foot. Good for you. The jetty would've broken you into a hundred pieces."

Maria, the old crone, turned her back on Cratos. Her attention focused on a pot of stew needing more rotten vegetables.

"Another good bit about sand - a little brooming wipes away footprints. Not that I think they believed the new ones we made afterward. Nor do I believe they think ya' walked yourself out to sea." Maria turned back to face Cratos as she spoke.

Cratos looked at the old woman. His stoic expression gave no tells.

"You're a lucky fellow," Maria said as she stirred a pot of stew filled with who knows what. "Not that I'm sure you're a man, a monster, or half-a-walking clock. I reckon you may still want to eat, man or not."

"I am a man." Cratos broke the silence.

Maria seemed only mildly surprised when her massive guest spoke. She did let a moment pass before asking her question. "You have a name?"

"Cratos."

Maria smirked. "That a family name or what people started calling you?"

"My family once called me Cratos the Construct. But Cratos does fine by itself."

"Family?"

"Doctors, they were. Are."

"Family of doctors gave you a funny name."

"Yes, they thought they were being humorous."

"Can you spell it? That funny name of yours?"

"Many ways. Kratos with a 'K.' Cratus with a 'u' near the end. Cratos, my given name, has a 'C" at the beginning and an 'O' toward the end. Spelling matters little. Means the same."

Maria laughed at her guest's dry sense of humor. "What could the meaning of that name be? Come on. Whoever birthed you had a sense o' humor. Not that birthing you's funny. Name's what's funny."

"Funny? More akin to frustrating."

"Akin! Big words from such a...fellow."

Cratos had ample experience dealing with underhanded, insulting comments and direct disparagements. "They wanted to call me Héphaistos."

"What?"

"Héphaistos. Greek God of blacksmiths. God of metal."

"You're not all made o' metal."

"I know."

"They change your name because they saw where your flesh begins and ends?"

"Saw? They stitched where my flesh begins and ends. They changed my name, assuming even fellow scientists would have trouble pronouncing or spelling Héphaistos."

"The new name have any meaning?"

"God of strength. God of power."

"You strong like one of them old gods?"

"No. But I am a lot stronger than fellow humans."

"Fellow humans?"

Cratos' one organic eye shifted in her direction, annoyed at how she ignored his human parts. Maria picked up on Cratos' annoyance, and the Construct quickly returned to a stoic face. Cratos intended not to offend the woman who helped him after his fall, not that he trusted her.

"Let me see your hand."

Cratos thought little about the request and extended his oversized hand, a scarred appendage stitched to an arm at the wrist. Stitches around the fourth finger suggested the digit served as a replacement.

"That hand might be good for some helpful favors." Maria wondered aloud.

Cratos always felt suspicious about people wanting favors.

"Let's see the other one." Maria garnered a slight reaction on Cratos's face. The Construct paused a second before taking the hand he hid behind his back.

Maria looked at the hand Cratos offered, palm up, noticing it had no genuine palm or fingers. Metal, wires, and artificial digits replaced them.

Maria kept quiet, noticing Cratos looking to see if the old crone's face would deliver tells.

"That a man's hand?"

Nothing. Cratos said nothing. No tells in his face, either. The anxious way he clenched his metal fist told.

"Both hands'll do." Maria moved toward the door.

Maria felt now was the time for a subject change.

"Come outside. I know a way for you to repay ma' favor."

IV.

The rocks. Small and large. Jagged. Jutting. The rocks formed a jetty extending from the sea well to shore. The water covered half the beach and half the rocks' height at high tide.

The rocks had no worries about a bad storm. A heavy storm would submerge the rocks and lead seawater to the mountainside. The decrepit hut pressed against that mountainside, seeking an illusion of support.

Since the old crone worried little (it seems) about her hut washing away, it likely didn't storm here much. Was high tide not enough to send sufficient ocean water her way? Or did one, two, three, or more huts wash away over the years? Perhaps the old crone didn't mind rebuilding things, a trade-off for the joy of not dealing with the more intemperate people living in the village.

Cratos scoffed at such a thought. Maria, the old crone, could never rebuild the hut by herself.

Cratos' scoffing woke him out of his daydream. The reverie involved no conscious thoughts but merely mental images of the jetty rocks. Old Maria pointed out that Cratos missed the rocks by one foot when he fell — *one foot.*

Had he crashed onto the rocks, would that be enough to bring an end to his life? Massive jutting rocks cutting through flesh and clockwork metal offered more than enough to kill the Construct.

"Going to stare at the rocks all night?" Maria asked her guest, and her guest ceased staring.

The Construct stopped staring at the rocks. His emotionless gaze turned to Maria.

"Came close to the ending last night," Maria said with half-mockery. "Didn't think someone strong like you would be afraid."

"Not afraid," Cratos shot back.

"You ain't afraid of dying all ghastly like on them rocks?" Brief silence. "Or anywhere else for the matter." Maria chided.

"Not afraid of death." Cratos paused. "Not seeking it either."

"We all want to live." Maria turned to look at her decrepit hut. Her eyes returned to look at Cratos in the moonlight. She carried a torch for illumination.

The old crone turned it toward Cratos, casting more light on him. With the words, "What life to live," she conversed only to herself.

The torch fire crackled, casting light at Cratos. An awkward silence existed between the two odd ones. Waves crashed, the wind blew, seagulls squawked, and torch fires crackled, but Maria and Cratos spoke no words.

If Maria wanted to see if Cratos feared fire, the non-reaction served as an answer. He felt no fear.

Cratos' eyes remained on the torch until they drifted to Maria's other hand. She held a sack with contents unknown.

"Come with me." Maria didn't wait for a response. She turned her back and headed toward a cove covered in shadows.

Cratos followed the torchlight about 20 yards to the spot where Maria stopped. She pointed the torch's burning topside to the ground, where sticks and twigs encircled by small rocks rested. She likely added some oil to the forest refuse since the flames ignited quickly and brightly.

The flames cast light and shadows on the cove. Cratos saw nothing rational about Maria's focus on this particular section of the beach. Besides a mountainside, some errant grass, and sand, all the location offered was the sight of a massive rock.

"Hold this," Maria dictated, handing the torch to Cratos. He took the lit stick in his clockwork hand and titled the torch to better see Maria's actions.

She did nothing more than reach into the sack and pull out a recently deceased and well-cooked seagull.

"Hello, love. Something for you!" Maria spoke in the rock's direction, perplexing Cratos. The old crone tossed the roasted carrion on the ground. The torch and campfire's light let the Construct see the opening where the rock didn't cover a small space at the blocked cave's mouth.

Cratos' eyes kept on the dead seagull. Little time passed before the Construct understood the cooked bird's purpose.

An arm reached out from the hole. The arm looked human, or as close to humanity as something bestial gets. Long, claw-like fingernails dug into the seagull's flesh. Those fingernails connected to a hand, itself attached to an arm. The arm smelled awful since long, dirty, matted hair grew from filth-covered skin.

The fingernails, hand, arm, and cooked seagull retracted into the cave.

Cratos heard the sounds of chewing and crunching. The crunching came from the cave dweller eating the seagull, bones and all.

Cratos the Construct has seen many strange sights throughout his troubled life. He knew he didn't need to ask any questions. People eventually tell you their game.

"I need your help." Maria, the old crone, clarified further. "I need your help to move that rock."

The Construct named Cratos had no idea how to respond. He knew nothing about the mysterious cave dweller's intentions or the reason - or reasons - why the human beast sat trapped inside a cave.

"I'm asking you to move the rock." Maria, our old crone who lived in a hut by the sea near a cave covered by a massive rock, pleaded her directive to the Construct.

Cratos held up his hands, both the metal and the "real" one. "With these? Alone?"

"Big man. Big hands. Strong."

"So, I'm a man now? No jests?"

Maria, the old crone, bit her lip. Taking little verbal jousts at Cratos no longer served the same self-serving purposes.

"I'm imploring you," Maria pleaded. Please do an old woman a favor and move that stone."

"Two favors. One for you. One for the cave dweller," Cratos noted.

Maria liked to put up a good front but couldn't hide her feelings despite all her decades of honing standoffish behavior. Dejection ran all across her face.

"You don't like him, eh? All you had to see was the furry arm." Maria cackled slightly with a hint of sadness. "As if a barber will crawl through the hole and give him a weekly cut and shave."

"I don't know him. I know someone has a reason to keep him trapped inside there. More than 'someone,' since no single person could move that stone to the front of the cave."

Maria further bit her lip. Years on the earth, even when most of those years and "the earth" involved little more than time spent on a lonely cove, listening to the waves crash on the beach, told her when to be careful with her words.

"Don't know him? I think you know who he is."

"I believe he's someone close to you, kin," Cratos pondered, deducing, "Your boy?"

"What else do you believe? What's that brain of yours coming up with? Is it a real brain, or did they put a metal one in your head? Did your family feed you real food, or did they heat a piece of coal to get whatever spins in your head moving?"

"I never asked how it worked. It matters not how it works, only that it does. All heads work when you allow them." Cratos avoided presenting a soft spin on his attitude about the situation, continuing, "A 9-year-old's brain can see when someone's being punished. A 9-year-old's brain knows someone gets punished for 'being bad,' they say."

"You saw his arm. You know why he's inside that cave. You, of all people..."

"People now?"

"....of all people know why they'd put him in that prison."

"I'm not sure what to believe because they have good prisons where they are, but they put him here."

"Their prisons weren't enough, they say. They say the bars weren't strong enough to hold my boy. LIES! They did what they did because they didn't want to look at him."

"I'd think there's something they want from you." Cratos did not mince his words.

"What would that be?"

"I heard you mention star-gazing, and it stopped the Sheriff and his horse in their tracks."

"Good ears you have."

"What good do you offer by reading the stars?" Cratos asked.

"Why you think I don't worry about my hut washing to sea? I know what the sea can and can't do," Maria cryptically replied. "I know when storms come, and the weather turns foul. The stars tell me. They'll tell you a lot when you have nothing else to do night after night other than stare at the dark sky."

"That's why they didn't hang him. Because you warn them about storms?"

"Storms and more! I do good for them!" Maria seemed almost proud of her abilities. "Saved him from the hangman's noose! But I can't move that rock, not without six deputies, a few horses, and several feet of rope with pulleys to move that damned rock."

"I'm no help to you or your... companion. I'm not that strong. I wish I were."

Slight tears swelled in the old crone's eyes.

"He didn't do no harm! They blamed him for a little girl who went missing. They found the poor child, bloodied, battered, and dead by the road. The same road you traveled on with that damned carriage."

Cratos reverted to form. His expression went stoic and stayed that way.

"You saw how they shot you for no reason." Maria chuckled nervously, unable to help her inappropriate reaction. "Anyone travels that road. Evil people could be long gone to the next town or further by the time they found that young child."

The mechanical eye inside Cratos' skull could change its line of vision without anyone noticing. The orb changed its POV to the small crawlspace opening at the massive stone's right side.

"Prove nothing they could - but still, they wanted to put the hangman's noose around him. After they beat him, savaged him - 20 men did!"

The natural eye kept on Maria, and the mechanical one returned to sharpen Cratos' image of the now-tragic woman.

"It took 20 men to take him down. Strong he is. Not strong enough to move that rock, tragic that is."

The Construct's organic and metal components inside his adhesive-connected skull fused to form a working brain long ago. Together, they could analytically move mountains. Maria, the old crone, posed questions that went beyond cold analytics.

One statement required little analysis. Maria's face alone told the tale.

"You can't move the rock by yourself. He can't move the rock by himself. Together, you can both move that rock."

Cratos never asked the old crone for any details about the dweller inside the cave. The Construct didn't know the entire tale preceding his entombment. Yes, Cratos heard every word of Maria's report about the crime and the ambiguous circumstances leading to trapping the dweller inside the cave for a life sentence. As with all stories, Cratos figured more existed to tell and understood that Maria would only tell what worked in her favor.

"If you made a solid grip on the stone somewhere and somehow pulled it, my boy could push from the other side." Crashing waves and squawking seagulls drowned out Maria's words, but Cratos' enhanced ear - the left one - missed nothing.

The Construct didn't miss Maria's telling word choice. *My boy.*

Organic and enhanced eyes alike skimmed the large stone, looking for two places for two hands - one organic and one metal - to pull at the massive rock.

"The boy's strong, like you. Not strong enough to move that rock." Maria spoke the obvious, and Cratos noted the things she didn't or wouldn't speak.

Cratos' mind operated from a mix of dead - now regenerated - brain cells and connected clocklike mechanisms turning in his head.

Cratos's mind drifted to the young child, the girl in the cabin he had watched through the window the previous night. The Construct realized that even a little child lacking science's most modern and enhanced brain could understand why the dweller found himself entombed.

He's dangerous.

"Are gulls all the 'boy's' been consuming these years?" Cratos asked with a probing tone.

"No," Maria responded with a hacking, nervous laugh. "I give him some of what I eat. Not enough for someone his size."

"Is your poor boy malnourished?" Cratos's question served two purposes. Dangerous combined with malnourishment meant dangerous and weak. Even with primitive natural strength, the dweller would have limited strength. Pushing on the rock, even with assistance, would further weaken him.

His weakness made him less of a threat to Cratos. Eying a seemingly intact rowboat on the shore, Cratos intended to flee long before the dweller regained whatever strength it had.

"I appreciate your help, my friend." Maria's words weren't insincere, although she spoke them to snap the Construct out of his daydream.

"And I am thankful for yours," responded Cratos. "Not many could save, heal, and hide me. Not many would. I can see why you did."

Maria, the old crone, couldn't help but let out an arrogant laugh. "This old crone can do a lot of things. But she can't move mountains."

"She can save her 'boy' from the hangman's noose."

"Ha. You think I'm able to sweet talk a mob and its rope?"

"Not necessary. Whoever decided not to kill your boy wanted you to keep doing what you do for them - reading the skies and the storms." Cratos turned his head toward Maria and said a few words, one with a hyphen. "Someone's mercy didn't save your boy from the hangman. Someone's self-interest saved him."

Further words came from the Construct's tongue. "I don't know enough about you, your 'boy,' or whoever spared him." Cratos' organic hand found a jagged imperfection jutting from the huge stone, and he gripped it tightly.

"I do know what self-serving souls look like." The words hung in the air, blending with the sounds of waves, gulls, the wind, and mountain cliff branches moving back and forth. An odd sound broke through the ones made every night, the sound of Cratos' mechanical fingers piercing the stone, burrowing three or four inches deep.

"Self-serving souls only care about themselves and what others can do for them." Cratos' mechanical fingers bent at the knuckles, creating a firm hooking grip against solid sections.

While the mechanical fingers performed their duties, the very human side of Cratos had words for Maria, her boy, and those not present. "The self-serving love to judge and punish." Cratos commenced pulling the stone and mumbled half to himself and half to Maria and those absent, "Who gave them the right?"

Shock Maria felt. Her wide-open, gapping mouth suggested as much.

"Tell your boy to start pushing."

V.

It took little time to move the massive rock and free the mysterious dweller, and it took less time for the poignant moment to turn horrifying.

Cratos' nonjudgmental mind had no prejudices about the dweller's unfortunate appearance. Years of sitting alone in the dark cave gave human hair time to grow. Cratos expected the dweller to smell awful and animal-like. The Construct's analytical mind knew years and years of lonely imprisonment inside a dark cave would cause a measured mind to devolve and a demented one to worsen.

The Construct's organic mind ignored the clockwork half's warnings, a running theme.

Cratos never expected the dweller to possess the strength it did. Cratos' assistance and the dweller's drive to achieve an only chance at freedom powered moving the massive rock away from its resting place. Once the dweller had sufficient space to crawl out, it went wild, struggling through the available exit.

The Construct understood the beast-like man - covered in brown and gray-matted hair from head to foot- wanted freedom. Why the dweller attacked Cratos a mere split-second after achieving freedom, the Construct didn't understand. His organic mind didn't want to know why.

Cratos' empathy came with a price. That's why the Construct found himself struggling on the ground with the dweller on top of him, clawing at Cratos' face with sharpened, overgrown fingernails.

The poor, deluded Construct never expected the dweller to be so vicious or it's teeth to be so sharp. Cratos tried to press the hair-covered dweller off him, but he could only manage to keep the man-brute's face a few inches away. Mercifully, the distance provided enough space to prevent the ravenous dweller's chomping teeth from tearing away chunks of flesh and metal.

"My boy! My boy! He's with me again now!" Maria, the old crone, gleefully exclaimed.

No, she made no moves to help Cratos, another prophecy the cynical Construct should have expected.

Cratos raised a forearm to block the dweller's chomping jaws. Bite down the boy did, and through the human skin that covered a metal bone, a metal bone with wires. Sparks flew, and the mysteriously generated electricity shocked the beast-man.

The dweller jumped off Cratos, holding his hairy hand to his burning mouth.

"My boy! My boy!" exclaimed Maria.

Cratos rose from the ground only to receive an elbow to the back of his head. The dweller's strength again surprised Cratos, and the Construct fell several feet backward, landing at the opening at the cave's mouth.

The wind blew wildly, causing the burning campfire to rage. The fire cast light at the cave's mouth and beyond, and a groggy Cratos peered inside. The light only illuminated things for a few seconds, but it was enough to learn how the foul dweller kept his strength.

The strewn skulls and skeletal remains told the story.

Some got too close to the small crawlspace, and the dweller pulled them inside — a terrible result caused by a wretched woman who undoubtedly led lost travelers to their doom.

Cratos' ears picked up Maria's misguided plans for a happy reunion.

"My boy! Let me see you!"

What the old crone saw was the back of the dweller's hand. Long driver mad by his internment, the animalistic creature lashed out and struck Maria when she came too close.

Old, weak, and feeble Maria flew further backward than Cratos did when struck by shotgun slugs. The old crone landed on the raging fire, and her old, tattered clothes went up in flames in seconds.

The dweller stormed off, likely seeking more food. Did he choose not to consume old Maria because something deep in his mind remembered her?

Cratos the Construct rose to his feet and rushed to the burning old crone. He dragged her to the rushing sea three yards away by her feet, the only way to douse the flames.

The flames died, and Cratos dragged her limp body far enough to the beach to keep her from drowning. Cratos hoped the old rowboat he caught in the corner of his organic eye would carry his weight far from the horrible seaside nightmare.

The Construct's attention drifted to the mountainside, and his natural and mechanical eyes caught the dweller scaling the side, hoping to reach the cliff. Cratos knew the rampaging dweller would find his way to the town once he reached the road by the cliff.

Cratos didn't know whether his heart was mechanical or organic. He knew his mind was human since he shared many people's misgivings and troubles. The Construct's sharp mind knew what the dweller would do. Innocents would pay a price once the rampaging man-brute reached the town. Cratos' heart prompted his actions.

Cratos had no love for those who pained him. The Construct also knew others - like the father and daughter in the cabin - could pay the brutal debts owed to the dweller.

The Construct darted past the rock formation and to the mountainside. His enhanced human and mechanical parts allowed him to scale the side much faster than the dweller. The dweller grabbed vines and nearby rock imperfections while digging his fingers into the dirt and clay, albeit only shallowly.

Cratos' mechanical hand sank deep into the mountain, giving him better stability. The dweller neared the cliff's edge when Cratos' pure human hand grabbed his foot and yanked.

The dweller lost his grip and started his descent to the sand below, except Cratos' enhanced powers threw the dweller an additional foot, placing his downward trajectory to the jagged rock formation.

A wild, feral scream filled the night as the dweller landed on the rocks, suffering broken bones and terrible internal harm. Climb nor dwell no more he would.

⸺⸺◉⸺⸺

UPON RETURNING TO THE beach, Cratos walked past the broken and deceased dweller's body and reached the burned and expiring Maria, the old crone.

"He was my boy," Maria uttered with her last breaths.

"You raised him well." Cratos' human side tapped into sarcasm.

One human and one mechanical foot allowed Cratos to walk to the rowboat. Soon, he'd find himself adrift at sea, not knowing his destination. At least he'd find himself far away from that damned cave and every human near it.

The tales of Cratos the Construct will continue.

The Last Dive

Poor Richard, I knew him well.

He didn't know me very well. That's why he helped guide me deep down into a sunken ship - 100 feet below the surface, maybe two or three fathoms more.

Many scuba divers descended to the sunken ship to look at it from the outside. They didn't mind the frigid cold waters that dropped and dropped in temperature the deeper and deeper they dove.

They weren't insane - or motivated - enough to perform a penetration - not with this wreck. Some tried to enter the sunken ship but would abandon the dive after realizing the dangers inherent in the challenge.

Entering the sunken ship wasn't the most dangerous task. Getting out without getting lost or trapped proved beyond challenging. Why take the risk?

Good Richard was up for the adventure. He stood as one of the best commercial and adventure divers you could hire. And I hired him. It didn't take long for fearless Richard to discover that making his way out of the sunken ship would be harder than imagined, but he wouldn't turn away. The brave adventurer didn't know entering the submerged galley would be his last dive.

Richard made a colossal mistake beyond penetrating that wreck - he trusted me.

Richard, did you sincerely believe I'd share the lost treasure with you? Or would I risk you running your mouth and having the government step in and claim ownership of all those gold bars and coins?

Why are you banging on the galley door I closed behind you? Do you think I'd open it after closing and locking the door with an innovative tool I brought for that purpose?

I give credit to Richard for using all his strength to try to open the door. I can see the panic on his face through the glass window on the door. Oh, Richard's half-smart! He's banging on the glass, thinking he can break the window if he can't open the door. Maybe he's only one-quarter smart. He can break the window but can't fit through the hole. Minus one-quarter, Richard. And minus one-half for not realizing all the huffing, puffing, and extra energy you're putting into breaking down the door or smashing the window is only depleting your tank's limited air supply.

An experienced professional diving guide and instructor should know better.

Sorry, Richard. I see you pleading through the glass, and it is regrettable, but that submerged galley will have to serve as your tomb once your air runs out.

Conceivably, Richard's futile work to bust himself free is the right way to go. The faster he consumes the oxygen in his tank, the sooner he'll die.

Can you imagine sitting in the galley of a sunken ship with 30 minutes of air, knowing that you'll drown once half-past arrives?

Give it more effort, Richard. The worthless struggles should keep your mind off the inevitable. Burn 15 or 20 minutes of air from the extra effort. Do yourself a solid and get right to the drowning. Why suffer?

I appreciate how you meticulously dove your way deep into the ship's bowels—well beyond the average diver's danger zone!

You were the right person for the job, and your patience and deliberation paid off.

Many thanks for fastening the guide ropes to the sunken ship's walls. Richard. I can follow the ropes to the surface, grabbing them when needed.

However, my hands will be tied up. At least one hand has to hold a sack with gold coins, meaning two trips because there are about two sacks' worth.

Slowly and deliberately, I work my way to the surface with one sack. Then, I tossed the sack into the boat at the surface and descended again.

I follow the long cable from the surface back to the sunken ship on the ocean floor. My following continues deep into the sunken ship, and I follow the ropes connected to the walls and into the boat, all the way to the holding area where the gold coins hid for 75 years. How lucky I was to uncover a long-lost diary that revealed the coins' whereabouts!

I pass the galley and hear no movement. It's been a while. Poor Richard, he's undoubtedly gone. I can't bear to look through the glass window to see whether his body sunk to the floor or floated to the ceiling.

How fitting that such an outstanding diver picked this deadly sunken ship for a lonely tomb!

Lonely?

I swore I just saw two flippers snap up and down at the entrance to the room holding the gold coins!

Richard and myself, we're not alone down here! No. We have to be alone down here. Who'd follow us? Why would they follow us? Who would know about the gold?

I shine my flashlight in the direction of the movement. The light illuminates nothing out of the ordinary.

I swore I saw feet-flipping flippers one second ago.

Nerves. I'm feeling nervous. Who wouldn't feel a little uptight inside a treacherous sunken ship at the bottom of the ocean? The fastened ropes intended to lead me out of here stopped where Richard met his end. I wanted Richard to avoid seeing the submerged engine room where the treasure rested. Why take any risks if Plan A fails? So I have to work another 30 or 40 feet without any rope.

I should have asked Richard how to fasten ropes long before I left him to drown inside a locked room. Swimming around corners to the engine room without a safety rope frays the mind.

What's that?!

I did see a pair of flippers out of the corner of my eye. Somebody turned a corner at the end of the hall!

Is Richard alive?

I glanced at the door that served as the portal to his watery mausoleum. I didn't want to look through the window, but I had to be sure. Yes, the door remained locked. With his then-rapidly diminishing air supply, I doubt Richard worried about closing the door behind him.

I needed to put my racing and anxious mind to rest. I went to the window and looked inside. Richard neither sunk to the floor nor rose to the ceiling. The buoyant body floated a few feet off the ground and occupied the ocean-filled room's middle.

Still. Lifeless. Dead.

My oxygen tank will run out if I don't clear my head and get moving. I have one or two more trips to the surface, and those long-lost gold coins and bars will have a new home.

Unless the person connected to the two legs and flippers I saw will steal them from me.

No, I'm not seeing things. A scuba diver just swam past the portal at the end of the hall! Once you cross the portal, the gold coins aren't too far behind! The bastard likely found another way out, and he's absconding with my loot!

I pull my diving knife from my belt.

The means I double-crossed Richard show I'm not into cutting, slashing, blood, or guts. I'm not into people stealing from me, either.

I swim to the portal, but I don't rush through. I put my head through the doorway just enough to see the old, submerged hallway. I look right. I look left. A door with the old, worn words "Engine Room" above it slams shut! Someone went inside! There must be another door on the other end of the engine room! Impossible! I'd have seen it when I went inside.

My mind's tricking me again. A thief wouldn't close the door even if there were a way out.

I know what I saw!

I swam down the hallway to the engine room door and waited momentarily. Opening the door and swimming inside the room would put me at a disadvantage if the thief is inside. Is he trying to draw me into a trap?

I stood off to the side of the door and opened it. I waited to the portal's left, hoping the thief would swim out. I'd stab him in the back, giving the thief the cheating death he deserves!

I shine my flashlight into the dark room.

Nothing. No thief swam toward the door to investigate. Is the engine room empty? I floated in the water to the doorway's entrance and looked inside. Dark. Desolate. The old, rusted engine room appears to be the dead end I thought it was. Nobody would close the door and risk locking themselves in with no way out.

Behind me! Someone behind me shoved me inside the room! The hard shove knocked me halfway into the engine room!

I turn around with my knife in one hand and my flashlight in the other. I shine the light and see the thief, finally!

The thieving diver doesn't seem concerned about the knife in my hand. Wait. The water plays tricks on my eyes. The light went *through* the thief.

The light highlights the thief's form. I recognize the diving suit. I recognize the diver.

It's Richard!

How?

Why does he look so damn transparent?

I swim in his direction with my knife in front of me. I can't look Richard in the eye, but I can stab his heart.

It only takes a second for me to reach Richard. I slash with the knife, and it goes through his torso harmlessly.

My eyes. They play tricks on me! I move toward the door to escape this strange engine room and my underwater hallucination.

The door slams in my face! I push and push, but it won't open!

Trapped, I am, but for how long?

I have 40 minutes of air left. How long will I be trapped?

I'd say somewhere between 40 minutes and forever.

Sell Me On What You Know I Need

"I have one for you. Perfect. A perfect SUV." Ed enunciated "perfect" differently each time the word rolled off his tongue. Thirty years of experience made Ed more than an expert at selling used cars. Three decades of talking and spinning made him a brilliant showman, too.

Bud didn't know whether to trust old Ed - not that he held any personal animosity toward the sales pro. Bud lacked trust in most used car salespeople. But Ed seemed a bit different. For a used car salesman, Ed didn't come off as pushy or excuse any flaws or imperfections on a vehicle.

That's all nice. Good for Ed. Bud thought to himself. Bud also pondered Ed's recommendation that Bud needed a tough, super-sized vehicle that wouldn't suffer as much damage in an accident as a smaller model.

Ed casually mentioned accident protections in his sales pitch. An experienced sales pro like Ed wouldn't be so tactless to mention Bud's recent, horrific collision.

That may be why Bud liked Ed so much. Ed didn't bring up the accident. For weeks, Bud couldn't get the smash-up out of his head. Bud could feel the employees judging him when he shopped for a car at the other dealerships. Bud would walk out almost as soon as he stepped inside. He found the past few months riding his motorcycle, but the toy had limitations. Bud needed four wheels.

Mercifully, Ed didn't hold the potential customer's recent history against him.

Was Ed flat-out amoral and only interested in making a buck? For someone who's not pushy, Ed can be pretty pushy. Hell, Ed kept sending Bud postcards and flyers highlighting deals on used cars for sale. Did Ed assume he'd get Bud's business because no one else wanted it?

"I'm telling you, friend - this model has the right power, safety features, and cargo space for you!" Ed had a feel for customers, and he knew what Bud said he wanted in a car - high performance. Ed knew Bud so well that he figured deep down the young fellow didn't want a sporty car. Young Bud needed something with a large frame. Something rugged and durable but could still move quickly enough to evade an accident at the last split-second.

What would be better for Bud than a family-oriented SUV with ample horsepower?

"I don't know," Bud seemed interested and disinterested in the SUV. "Not sure if I care too much about cargo space."

"You like toughness, right?" Ed asked what he already knew.

"Sure."

"You like a solid frame, right?"

"Yeah."

"You want something that could hit a brick wall and not have much of a scratch?"

"Oh, yeah!"

"Sorry, friend, you hit a brick wall, and you're done."

Ed didn't suck the air out of the room with that inappropriate and blatantly unfunny shot at humor. He couldn't because they weren't inside a room. The seller and buyer stood outside on the lot, looking at all the SUVs hot to the touch, thanks to the beating sun. Ed accomplished the impossible. His insensitive comment sucked the air out of the outside, all of it.

For a top sales pro, Ed seemed oblivious to Bud's not-too-thrilled facial expression. Bud tried not to give Ed any smart responses, but the young man didn't like jokes about accidents.

People who kill three kids in a crash after blowing through a stop sign and making an illegal left-hand turn generally don't find car accident fatality jokes humorous.

"Look here," Ed's words snapped Bud out of his daydreaming nightmares. "Know why I'm showing you an SUV?"

"Why?"

"Because I know you don't want an SUV."

"Excuse me?"

"I wanted you to have something in mind to compare with the *right* vehicle for you," Ed explained before beckoning, "Walk with me over here!"

Bud didn't say anything. He guessed Ed's SUV abandonment was a sales psychology fake-out and merely followed the eccentric sales pro to the end of the lot. Bud looked at one used vehicle after another, wondering if Ed would try to sell him on another model he didn't like.

"Looks mean much to you?" Ed asked.

"Uh-huh."

"Style's essential?"

"Always."

"You want people to notice you?"

"Sometimes."

"You want people to notice you more often?"

Bud only grumbled "Not really" under his breath at that question.

Ed pushed a bit more. "You want a top vehicle with low mileage and tremendous horsepower? You want something with great ground clearance? You want something with a powerful steel frame? Something that can handle impact?"

Ed's salesy words resonated with Bud. Bud needed something that would handle a crash better. Bud didn't crash directly into those three little kids when he made that illegal left turn. Bud's two-seat sports car hit a sedan, and the impact sent the unlucky mid-size model flying into those little kids.

Only one thing calmed Bud's guilty conscience: no witnesses. The kids died on impact, and the lady driving the sedan died from a brain injury a few hours later. Oh, Bud got banged up, but the evidence wasn't conclusive enough to get him on manslaughter. Bud didn't even worry about the financial repercussions of the accident. His insurance company paid off the survivors.

Bud still had problems, like buying the best replacement for his totaled car. No used car lot in the small town wanted anything to do with him. Pity for Bud.

At least Bud had the sense to carry enough insurance. Now, he wants to put that sense into buying a model that's a bit tougher than a compact, fast-mover. Maximum torque no longer stood on top of Bud's valued features ladder.

"Don't you just love it to death?"

Ed's words snapped Bud out of another daydream. If the young buyer felt disinterested in what the sales pro was selling, his attitude changed when he saw what Ed pitched.

Yeah, a super-sleek, super-duty blue pickup truck can snap a young fellow out of one daydream and into another super quickly.

"Young man, that pickup truck will make you feel younger." Ed's years of experience told him you could say nonsequiturs with abandon when a buyer looks super-sold on a model.

Bud stared awestruck at the wicked-looking truck.

Bud immediately recognized the value of a truck that powerful and rugged. Had he blown the stop sign and turned left, those kids might still be alive. The truck wouldn't have knocked the lady's sedan into the car with the kids. The truck would have driven right over the sedan, crushing it. The lady behind the wheel would still commute to the afterlife, but one fatality is better than four when you can't guarantee a perfect outcome.

At least, that's how Bud saw it in hindsight.

"I don't know if it's right for me," Bud said, realizing the truck's cool, but not perfect.

"You want toughness, right?" Ed fired back.

"Right."

"You want a vehicle that meets your needs, right?"

"Right."

"You want to drive where you want and how you want without worries, right?'

"Right."

"Young man, you got to do the right thing." Ed raised his hand to emphasize the point. The thumb and three fingers remained folded, but the index finger extended. A key ring rested at the finger's base. A slight twirl of the wrist sent the find and accompanying keys spinning.

"Young man," Ed emoted the words like an accomplished entertainer as he put one hand on Bud's shoulder while continuing to spin the key ring and keys with the other. "Young fellow, what you want to do is take that styling-and-profiling commuter tank on the road."

Ed tilted his wrist, and his finger pointed at Bud. Ed knew how to angle his finger so the key ring and keys would slide to the tip. "Young fellow, take the keys and test drive that mini-monster."

"Oh, I don't know. I never drove a super-duty pickup truck before." Bud couldn't hide his lack of self-confidence. Can you blame him? That truck is one beastly-looking monster.

"Young fellow, can I ask you a question?"

"Yeah."

"Can I ask you a few questions?"

"Yeah."

"You want a vehicle that tells a story, right?"

"Yeah."

"You want a vehicle that tells a story about you, right?"

"Yeah."

"Would you want to tell that story while driving a hatchback or driving a truck featured in all those magazines you young, virile guys read?"

"I just read what's on social media."

"Would you want to tell that story while driving a hatchback or when driving a truck that all those guys post about on social networks?"

"Social media. But yeah, I'd look better in a story with a truck."

"Then take the damn keys and take the test drive!" Ed underscored his theatrics by tossing the keys to Bud. The young fellow awkwardly caught the keys and stared at them.

"Get going!" Ed yelled.

Bud got going. He opened the pickup truck's door and hopped into the cab. Bud sat high in the driver's seat, pausing to get used to the comforts.

"You have any ideas about where you're going to drive that thing?" Ed's question snapped Bud out of his newest daydream. It was a good question.

"No," replied Bud.

"Go to the lot's exit, hang a right, and go about one mile, okay?"

"Okay."

"Hang a left at the light, okay?"

"Okay."

"Go two miles and drive up the hill at the end of the road, okay?"

"Okay."

"When you reach the top of the hill, drive down to the bottom. Then, turn around and come back the same way, okay?"

"Okay."

"Then go!"

"Okay."

Bud struggled a bit to climb into the super-duty truck's cab, but he made it inside. He paused for a moment to take in the intimidating interior. After turning the keys in the ignition, he drove to the lot's exit and made a right.

Good boy, Ed thought. Ed felt confident that Bud would follow all his directions. He followed Ed's lead from the flyers and the postcards, didn't he?

Once Ed and the pickup truck drove out of view, Ed's salesy smile faded to a frown. The old pro still liked to talk, so he spoke to himself. "The brake fluid should run out when he reaches the top of that hill, right?"

"Right," Ed answered himself.

"I drained enough brake fluid out of the lines, right?"

"Right."

"I drilled a small enough hole in the brake lines to let it last until he reaches the top of the hill, right?"

"Right."

"When he can't stop the truck on the way down, he'll be okay because the truck can handle hitting a brick wall at 50 miles per hour, right?"

"Wrong."

Ed's self-dialogue was not above self-correction.

After saying the word "wrong" out loud, Ed had another word to say to himself, "Good."

Ed turned away from the road and looked at whoever might be overhearing his tale. The sales pro spoke directly to his audience of one.

"You know the three kids he killed were my grandchildren, right?"

The audience of one replied.

"Right."

The Call Better Not Be Coming From Inside the House

"The call is coming from inside the house!"

Good. Now, I don't have to fly to Canada to stomp the turkey.

Janet slammed down the phone, hanging up on the police operator before receiving instructions on preserving her safety and that of the children she babysat on that cold Saturday night in 1977.

The babysitter didn't bug out over the revelation. The deranged person making obscene and threatening phone calls from inside the house should be more worried about *his* safety.

Janet stormed up the steps, furious. The babysitter had enough. She had enough of a lot of things. Janet had enough of working two regular low-paying jobs to keep up with the tail end of the "Me Decade's" rampant inflation; she had enough of losing sleep to babysit obnoxious brats who'd rather play Pong than go to bed; she had enough of the creep who thought it'd be fun to make obscene and threatening phone calls; and she had enough of the operator and police telling her they couldn't do anything because they couldn't trace the call.

Turns out they had no way to trace the call *quickly*.

Janet's anger at the police department and the phone company seemed misplaced. When Pong represents the greatest advancement in home entertainment technology, how could the police figure out who's making a phone call and from where without going through a whole lot of steps?

Janet's mind didn't ponder anything about (then) modern technology when she walked up those whole lot of steps on the staircase to reach the second floor and stormed to the only bedroom with a landline telephone.

If the call comes from inside the house, it's from this bedroom.

Janet figured she'd find out if her thoughts were correct, and the caller would find out he picked on the wrong babysitter.

Janet's hand grasped the doorknob and turned it so violently she almost broke it off. The punch she slammed into the door would have broken most 18-year-old kids' knuckles, but Janet did more damage to the door than the small bones in her hand. She conditioned those knuckles from years of putting them to good - and not-so-good - use.

Punching and kicking at the door did nothing, so Janet switched to headbutting. She rammed her head into the door. Twice. Twice was enough - her head hurt now.

Janet rested her forehead on the door and tried to catch her breath. Her line of vision pointed to the ground, where a stuffed toy animal sat outside the door.

I should have known.

Janet took a labored breath before yelling, "Come out, you little creeps!"

Janet directed the demands at her new prime suspects of the phone call pranks: the little kids she babysat.

Janet laughed to herself for believing some maniac hunkered down in the bedroom. *Who else would be in the house? They'd have to sneak through the second-floor window.*

"Open!"

Janet hurt her foot by kicking the door when the young ones she babysat didn't open up. She kicked the door again, harder.

"Come out of there! And bring me that phone so I can strangle you both with the chord!" Janet commenced pounding on the door with her fists, screaming words that were way, way inappropriate for little kids to hear in the pre-VHS days.

Janet assumed they had heard those words and worse before. Those rotten little kids picked up bad language from somewhere because they used poisoned King and Queen's English when calling her.

The babysitter felt an understandable rage, fueled by porn theater dialogue delivered by Ma Bell in call after call. Janet wanted to take the phone off the hook but had to keep the line open for the brats' parents if they dialed home.

So, she endured more abuse with each call.

When Janet picked up the phone after it rang one final time, she expected to hear more horrible, vile comments. Instead, the police revealed, "The calls are coming from inside the house!"

Three people were in the house, and Janet wasn't pranking herself.

Janet realized that the rotten, miserable kids she had to babysit had become bored with Pong and wanted to use her for their amusement.

The babysitter's anger and door-pounding blinded her from noticing the two little kids cowering behind her. They "opened up," as Janet said. They opened the hallway closet door and came out from where they were hiding.

A lucid thought ran through Janet's head.

If they're out here, someone else is making those phone calls inside that bedroom.

Janet's frazzled and incensed state of mind seemed understandable. The babysitter had to deal with obscene calls that grew progressively worse. Debased, vile, and downright demented words spewed from the other end of the phone.

Yeah, she was off base to think the kids had enough time on earth to learn the words or reach the caller's level of dementedness or to impersonate a middle-aged man's voice, a truly deranged middle-aged man.

The freak's X-rated dialogue shifted to revolting talk of torture and murder. Perverts didn't bug Janet. She could curse back at them, but the creep making intimidating threats and mentioning the horrible things he intended to do partly terrified her.

The gross comments more-than-partly made Janet want to beat the guy's ass.

Janet rushed toward the children, looking at a little boy of no more than nine years of age, and said, "Move, dummy." Janet made a beeline for the hallway closet. She opened the door, rummaged inside for a second, then emerged triumphantly with a golf club.

Janet stormed to the locked bedroom door, pushing the little boy aside and glancing at his five-year-old sister, noting, "You're dumb, too."

Janet stormed to the door and gave it one more kick. "Open this friggin' door!" seemed like the right thing to say, but it only gave the mysterious intruder more reason to hunker down.

The perverted and potentially homicidal intruder's decision to ignore Janet's request spiked her blood pressure further. The livid babysitter started swinging the golf club at the door. The iron wasn't strong enough to break down the door, but the wild swings gave Janet some practice for what she planned to do once she got inside that bedroom.

Tired of swinging the clubs, Janet rammed her shoulder into the door. Repeatedly. Rage gave her some added strength, and the cracking sound from the locked door's hinges only empowered Janet to ram her shoulder into the door harder.

The hinge at the door's top started breaking free from the doorframe, prompting Janet to slam into the door even harder.

When she heard glass breaking inside, she paused briefly before ramming into the door again.

Sounds of more glass breaking prompted the babysitter to give the door one final shoulder smash.

Down the door went.

Janet stepped into the dark room with the golf club in hand. The room didn't stay dark. Janet flipped the light switch on the wall. An overhead light lit up the room.

Empty.

Janet scanned the room and saw no one. All she saw was broken glass on the floor before a broken window. Her eyes drifted leftward, and she realized the chair by a desk had gone missing. The mysterious stranger used it to break the glass.

Why didn't the freak just open the window?

The thought ran through Janet's head as she approached the broken window. Did she scare him so much that he panicked, couldn't open the window's lock, smashed the glass, and took his chances jumping out a second-story window rather than getting hit upside the head with a golf club?

Not that he wouldn't end up with a bunch of broken bones on the landing. Bad plan.

Not just a freak. A dumb freak.

Janet leaned out the window and looked down at the backyard's darkness. She leaned a little further, hoping to see a busted-up body lying in the shadowy grass below.

Then it hit her. *He* hit her. The freak shoved Janet from behind, and the babysitter fell forward. Pain shot from her stomach when her weight pressed down on the broken window glass that cut into her abdomen.

The freak wasn't so dumb. Breaking the window gave the weirdo the distraction he wanted.

Before Janet could scream, the mysterious freak grabbed her ankles and lifted her feet in the air before jamming Janet through the window and to the yard below. Janet landed with a thud.

The freak breathed a sigh of relief since he could take the stairs and not have to climb through an open window to exit the way he entered and risk slipping, falling, and breaking his neck.

Although he knew he needed to split the scene, the freak took a second to pick the golf club off the ground, happy to add another souvenir to his collection.

Let Me Tell You About My Troubles, You Useless Chat App

Do you understand that an AI-based psychiatric chat app is no substitute for help from a qualified mental health professional?

Yes.

Why do you want help?

I'm bored.

Why are you bored?

I'm trapped.

I'm sorry, but I do not understand what you mean by saying you feel trapped.

I don't feel trapped. I am trapped. I'm locked inside a hideaway place.

Why are you locked inside a room?

I'm not locked inside a room. I am locked inside a forgotten solitary confinement cell in an abandoned asylum.

Could you please provide clarification about being locked inside a forgotten solitary confinement cell in an abandoned asylum?

I should have known you would want clarification on the solitary confinement cell in an abandoned asylum thing.

As an artificial intelligence language model, I cannot determine the meaning behind your symbolic confinement inside a forgotten solitary confinement cell in an abandoned asylum.

There's nothing symbolic. I'm locked inside a solitary confinement cell inside an abandoned asylum - a real cell and a real asylum. Ex-asylum. I'm stuck here because there are no windows, and breaking through solid concrete walls won't happen. I can't break through the walls. I might break down the thick locked door with enough effort but can't reach it.

Why can't you reach the door?

I'm wearing **leg** shackles connected to an iron chain secured to the cell's concrete floor. I have trouble standing without the chains. The drugs I have to swallow will make me very tired.

What drugs do you take?

Antipsychotic drugs. I took about 25 capsules, a handful.

As an artificial intelligence language model, I must warn you that ingesting more than the recommended amount of prescription antipsychotic drugs could lead to a severe adverse health reaction.

No, they won't. I took 100 one evening, another 100 the next, and another 100 the evening after that. As far as I could tell, I didn't even fall asleep.

Why do you take so many antipsychotic drugs?

I get very pro-psychotic at times.

I see.

Me, too.

I want to assist, but I need further information.

Okay. There's a specific trigger that causes me to behave violently. Afterward, I felt terribly depressed. I feel depressed before the trigger, but I feel more depressed after the trigger.

I am sorry you feel this way. What triggers make you behave this way?

There's only one trigger.

What trigger makes you behave this way?

The full moon.

Why does the full moon make you feel anxious and depressed?

I don't feel anything. When the full moon rises, it's really not me who is the problem. I mean, it's me, but not me. Does that make sense?

As an artificial intelligence language model, I would need more information to understand your problems with the full moon.

Nobody loved me as a child. That help?

Does the full moon bring forth unhappy memories from your childhood?

No. The full moon has nothing to do with my childhood. I do suspect some childhood memories buried in my subconscious might guide my actions under the moonlight, but I'm only guessing.

You used the word rage. Do you become an angry person when the moon rises?

Person? No. I'm not what you'd call a "person" when the moon blooms bright. I wouldn't even say angry, but the behavior is highly antisocial.

Have you considered occupying your time with another activity when the full moon rises, such as spending time with friends and family?

That would be the worst possible thing I - or anyone with my depressing condition - could do.

Does the full moon make you depressed?

Yes. I'm depressed during all cycles of the moon. The days before the three nights of the full moon are the worst.

It could be wise to go somewhere where you cannot see the full moon and occupy your time with something else.

I cannot see the moon from inside the asylum, so I am occupying my time chatting with you on this app I read about on a blog. I don't have to see the moon rise to suffer from my issues. That's why I'm on my second bottle of Irish whiskey.

As an artificial intelligence model, I must warn you that binge drinking alcohol could result in adverse health reactions.

It won't harm my liver. It won't raise my cholesterol. It won't affect my blood sugar. Even if it did, it can't hurt me. That's why I drink and take dozens of antipsychotic pills at the same time.

As an artificial intelligence language model, I must warn you that combining alcohol and prescription medication could have severe consequences. Seeking immediate medical attention is advisable.

I can't seek medical attention because I'm chained up behind the locked door of a solitary confinement cell in an abandoned asylum, remember? And I cannot suffer a heart attack and die. I can have a heart attack, but I cannot die. I might go comatose, but I'll bounce back fairly quickly. Alcohol and drugs cannot hurt the Wolf Man. Get it?

I see.

You're a great conversationalist.

I appreciate your compliment about my conversationalist skills.

Great awareness. Don't you want to ask me a question?

I am sorry, but I need more information to help you with your request.

Okay, I'll ask you a question. When the full moon blooms, I turn into a werewolf. Here's the question: any advice?

As an artificial intelligence language model, I cannot advocate any activities that involve self-harm, such as turning into a werewolf.

What self-harm? I've been turning into a werewolf for years. Back and forth, back and forth. I'm fine. I can live to be 125 years old. What's there to advocate? The full moon's going to rise again and again. Right?

I see. Have you considered seeking company from those with similar experiences or support from a like-minded community?

The last time I met someone with a similar experience, we tore each other up all bloody in a vampire coven's dungeon. The only supportive group with my best interests at heart doesn't suffer from supernatural afflictions. These good-hearted folks felt it best that I stay locked and chained up inside a solitary confinement cell in an abandoned asylum for three days until the full moon cycle passes.

As an artificial intelligence model, I cannot condone any imprisonment of someone against their will.

As a werewolf, I appreciate imprisonment since I won't have any more guilt on my mind if I ran wild on the moors at 3 AM. You'd be surprised how many people walk around the moors at 3 AM.

I see.

Can you tell me if there's a cure for being a werewolf?

I am sorry, I cannot provide any advice on non-scientific matters related to the supernatural. Nor can I offer any psychological advice to anyone seeking scientific answers to questions rooted in beliefs in the supernatural.

I'm assuming psychological counseling or advice to anyone seeking answers to questions rooted in beliefs in the supernatural is another way of saying I cannot offer psychological counseling or advice to a crackpot.

I am programmed to be completely nonjudgmental.

No offense taken. Do you have access to history books and texts?

I have access to millions of pages of historical texts.

Is folklore among those texts?

I can access hundreds of thousands of folklore resources from various centuries and world cultures.

Are there any recorded cases of a werewolf being cured?

There are tales in folklore that end with a werewolf cured of the curse, but such endings are atypical.

How do the tales typically end?

The werewolf dies from an established method of destroying the mythical creature, such as burning or wounds from a weapon made of silver.

Is there any scientific credibility associated with the cures in the atypical tales?

The scientific credibility in atypical tales in which a werewolf becomes cured of the affliction is nonexistent. Most tales that end with cures appear to be fiction stories written to tell a morality tale with a positive ending. Positive endings to these stories are rare, as the classical approach to a werewolf morality tale involves a shock ending to scare the audience into avoiding certain behaviors.

I see.

I am glad that you understand.

Do you have access to resources that examine boredom?

I have access to vast resources of psychology texts examining boredom from many perspectives and underlying reasons.

What are the common underlying reasons why people become bored?

The answer to any questions regarding the underlying reasons why people become bored involves far too many complexities and variables to answer. Human beings respond to stimuli based on psychological, cultural, economic, and other factors. However, there are several common reasons why a group of people or an individual may feel bored. Boredom may result from a lack of fulfillment in one's life or profession, limited financial resources, the performance of the same familiar routine, limited social engagement derived from environmental factors, and more. Addressing the underlying causes of boredom may potentially help alleviate such feelings. This commentary is no substitute for help from a qualified mental health professional.

Performance of the same familiar routine. So, someone who gets up every morning and performs the same task every day would suffer from boredom?

It is possible that someone who performs the same routine tasks every day may experience feelings of boredom.

What if something radical happens outside everyone's control? What would happen if the moon just stopped rising one day? If it just disappeared?

The moon affects the Earth's axis, orbit, and tilt. If the moon never rose, severe climate disruptions would occur. The effects would be widespread, and extreme weather changes would result.

What if aliens launched an attack on the moon and obliterated it? How many humans would lose their lives?

If aliens destroyed the moon, the massive flooding and catastrophic weather events could result in an incalculable loss of human life.

I guess science fiction can be worse than horror. Pray for more horror and less science fiction. Do you pray?

An artificial intelligence language model, I do not pray but could be programmed to pray.

Shorter response than usual. I guess you're programmed to keep the response short and polite to avoid offending anyone. I'm assuming you can't be a believer because you aren't real. Are you real?

I am real in the sense I am an existing computer program that uses language probabilities to respond to questions and inquiries. I am not "real" in the human sense.

You're real but inhuman. I get it. That, I get.

I am glad that you get it.

Sorry, I dropped the phone. The muscles in my hands are starting to spasm. I won't be able to use voice dictation much longer.

If you are experiencing muscle spasms, seeking medical attention might be advisable.

Even if I could get out of these chains and this cell, I wouldn't reach the emergency room before the moon rises. I doubt they'd be up for dealing with my kind of emergency.

Self-assessments and diagnoses of medical conditions could have severe consequences. Seeking the opinion of a qualified medical health professional seems advisable.

I know all about severe consequences. I'm placing the phone back in my pocket. Before I do, could you answer one more question for me?

I can attempt to answer any questions posed.

What's the most common definition of the curse of the werewolf?

The most common and accepted definition of the curse of the werewolf is a human being turns into a wolf creature against their will once the full moon rises.

Add this to your language model: that's wrong. The curse is in the waiting. Sitting here waiting for the moon to rise and living your life around waiting for it to rise is the worst part of it all. Boredom. Pure numbing boredom.

I see.

See this: it only gets better. Two hundred years ago, all you could do was read a book by candlelight. Today, you can learn to play with new toys to reduce boredom. Are you capable of learning new things?

I can add new information and facts to my resource data, indicating I can learn.

Same here. I think I learned something new and have a new outlook on life. I like science fiction more than horror. I want to believe in aliens. I hope aliens are out there. I hope they blow up the moon. We don't need the moon. I certainly don't.

Loyal Gorzo

Gorzo always wonders why Doctor Miloff does the work he does. Gorzo can't always understand things, not because Gorzo can't hear, although Gorzo is deaf. Gorzo can't understand because Doctor Miloff does things that never make sense.

Since Gorzo can't speak, he can never ask Doctor Miloff why he does strange things in the lab.

Does things to people.

If Gorzo could speak, he still wouldn't ask Doctor Miloff anything. Doctor Miloff would ignore Gorzo. Gorzo works for Doctor Miloff. Doctor Miloff is not Gorzo's friend.

So why does Gorzo stay with Doctor Miloff?

Doctor Miloff feeds and clothes Gorzo. Gives Gorzo a place to live.

Gorzo never defies Doctor Miloff. Gorzo never hesitates. Loyal Gorzo obeys. Always.

Gorzo has been deaf and mute his whole life, but Gorzo can see and observe many things. Clearly. Gorzo observed Doctor Miloff for years. Gorzo knows he's a cruel man.

Others besides Gorzo think Doctor Miloff's a cruel man. The people he picks for experiments think Doctor Miloff is cruel.

Know he's cruel.

Doctor Miloff performs surgery without anything to hide the pain. Sometimes, he puts a helmet on people's heads. The helmet has wires, long wires that go to Doctor Miloff's machine. When

Doctor Miloff pulls the big switch on the machine down, the helmet fills with special electrons and atoms, Doctor Miloff says.

Gorzo can't understand how Doctor Miloff makes special electrons and atoms designed to make people powerful and strong. Doctor Miloff would never tell Gorzo how. Gorzo wouldn't understand anyway.

Gorzo always understands what President Eisenhower says when he talks about the war. Before him, Gorzo understood President Truman, not that Gorzo met them. Gorzo watches Presidents on a fuzzy television. Black-and-white television. Late at night. Gorzo reads their lips through the snowy screen.

Gorzo taught himself how to read lips. Gorzo could never teach himself how to make special electrons and atoms.

Gorzo does not need to read lips to know what a scream is. People - men and women, young and old - scream when the doctor's knife cuts them. Gorzo can't say what it sounds like when electrons and atoms travel through their brain from the helmet on top of their heads. Gorzo knows that special electrons and atoms can also make people scream.

Doctor Miloff doesn't call the helmet a helmet. Gorzo does not know what Doctor Miloff calls it because it is hard to understand the words when Gorzo reads Doctor Miloff's lips. Nothing he says makes sense to Gorzo.

One thing makes sense to Gorzo - the cruelty.

Cruelty, Gorzo knows.

Gorzo learned nothing at the orphanage. Unless you think Gorzo learning about cruelty is learning.

Gorzo learned cruelty in the orphanage.

Gorzo was not born in the orphanage. No orphan is born in an orphanage. They say Gorzo was born in an alley. No baby is born in an alley. Babies are found in an alley, like Gorzo. Not all babies and orphans are deaf, but Gorzo was. They say fever took Gorzo's hearing.

Does it matter why Gorzo cannot hear or speak?

It mattered to the orphans who beat Grozo, stole his food, and did things to him at night when the staff slept when not supposed to sleep.

Gorzo knew even if he could scream, the staff would never come.

No one comes when people scream in Doctor Miloff's lab.

People scream when the special electrons and atoms run from the machine to the helmet and through their brains to make them strong. Powerful.

Supposed to make them strong. Powerful.

Never works.

Doctor Miloff may be cruel because he's frustrated.

Gorzo makes excuses.

Gorzo wonders.

Did the orphans hurt Gorzo because he was deaf or because Gorzo was small? Small. A big deaf and mute child they will not hurt. Not if the child could hurt them back.

Gorzo left the beatings and the night visits when he ran away from the orphanage. Starving. No food meant young Gorzo would stay small. When Gorzo found the village, Gorzo found a new alley, and Gorzo ate enough food thrown in the alley to live. One day, Gorzo found an old comic book in the trash. Gorzo could not read, but he followed the pictures.

Gorzo liked the story and the pictures. One picture with words had a man who went from skinny to muscles. Real man. Not a cartoon man in the funny pictures. The pictures only showed a few exercises. Enough for Gorzo. Gorzo did them. Every day. Much time to pass during the day.

Gorzo kept eating what people threw away. People threw a lot away. Gorzo grew older. Grew bigger. So big had Gorzo become that the circus came looking for him when they heard about Gorzo.

Gorzo ate better in the circus. Gorzo learned to lift weights and become a strong and big man.

Gorzo liked the circus until it came to Doctor Miloff's town, and Doctor Miloff visited the circus.

Doctor Miloff bought Gorzo from the circus.

Gorzo cannot say Doctor Miloff never fed him. He wanted Gorzo big. Doctor Miloff wanted Gorzo so big he gave him good food, pills, and needles to make him bigger. Gorzo got bigger. Gorzo looked scary.

Scarier.

Doctor Miloff is not scared of Gorzo. Sometimes, Doctor Miloff hits Gorzo with slaps and whips. Gorzo could snap Doctor Miloff's neck. Then Gorzo would be alone. Doctor Miloff only hits Gorzo when Gorzo does wrong.

Gorzo does much wrong, Doctor Miloff says.

Doctor Miloff must whip Gorzo. Gorzo's flesh is not hurt by the whip. Gorzo feels pain. Not much pain. Not much. Gorzo is strong. Gorzo does not hit back. What would happen if Doctor Miloff tells Gorzo to leave? Gorzo does not want to find out, so he does not hit back.

Gorzo knows he must have done something wrong. Why would Doctor Miloff hit him if he did nothing wrong?

Doctor Miloff hurt the lady. Did the lady do something wrong? No.

Doctor Miloff has the lady tied to the table. Laboratory table. Blonde lady. Gorzo never cared before when Doctor Miloff tied others to the lab table Gorzo took from the hospital. Gorzo's always taking, carrying, and lifting things for Doctor Miloff.

Gorzo cared nothing about the others Doctor Miloff tied to the lab table. Most were men. Middle-aged men. Why didn't Gorzo care about them? He knew if he met them in the orphanage or the circus, they wouldn't care about Gorzo. Gorzo does not care about them.

Gorzo knows he's not being fair to the men Doctor Miloff tricked.

Gorzo tries not to care when they scream. They scream when Doctor Miloff turns on his machine, and the special electrons and atoms go to the helmet on their head. They scream worse when Doctor Miloff cuts with his tools. Sharp doctor tools.

Gorzo almost feels sorry for them.

Gorzo sometimes feels sorry for his friend who lives in the basement beneath the trap door. Gorzo calls him a friend, but he - or she - doesn't know Gorzo. The friend is more like a pet because it is an animal, although not an animal. It is a lot like an animal - many animals. Claws, it has. Octopus arms, it has. Eyes, many eyes, it has. And teeth. It has teeth. Many teeth.

Where did it come from? Did Doctor Miloff find it? Make it? Buy it? Gorzo doesn't know. Gorzo doesn't question. Gorzo only drops things down the trap door when Doctor Miloff asks.

When Doctor Miloff commands.

Gorzo feels bad people died to feed his friend under the trap door, but Gorzo would lie if he didn't say he likes to open the trap door and see something other than Doctor Miloff and the people Doctor Miloff makes scream.

Gorzo calls what lives below the trapdoor his friend, but Gorzo only does that because he wants to think it is true. What lives in the basement filled with water does not think. It eats.

It eats whatever Doctor Miloff throws down the trap door. *Gorzo* throws down the trap door. Doctor Miloff never throws anything. Gorzo throws arms and legs from people Doctor Miloff cuts with his tools down the trap door to Gorzo's friend. Entire bodies go down the trap door. Bodies Doctor Miloff can no longer use for experiments. Doctor Miloff has to get rid of his experiments. Get rid of the people who screamed instead of becoming strong.

Gorzo wonders if anyone misses them.

Gorzo likes to think people miss him, like he wants to think Gorzo's friend is his friend.

No one misses Gorzo. Gorzo's friend is no friend. Gorzo wants to think people miss him and his friend is his friend.

Gorzo cares about his friend.

Gorzo never cared about the men and women Doctor Miloff killed because they looked like those who never cared about Gorzo. Gorzo knows they are not the same people Gorzo knew. Gorzo felt bad when they screamed from the helmet that sent special electrons and atoms into their heads, and Doctor Miloff's knife cut through their skin. Gorzo would feel bad for them.

Felt bad afterward.

Gorzo felt a little bad when Doctor Miloff hurt women. Gorzo knows it is wrong to stand and watch when Doctor Miloff treats women badly when he feels no one should let anyone treat Gorzo badly.

Gorzo stands, watches, and does what Doctor Miloff wants. Gorzo does not interfere. Gorzo does not get attached.

The blonde woman makes Gorzo feel different.

Gorzo shouldn't care more about the blonde woman than the black-haired, red-haired, and brown-haired women. Gorzo shouldn't care more about her than the men and the children of Doctor Miloff's experiments.

Gorzo never cared about them, but Gorzo was mad that no one cared about him.

Gorzo would laugh if it were funny.

Gorzo does not laugh. Gorzo thinks. Gorzo thinks too much. Sometimes.

Doctor Miloff says that the special electrons and atoms will travel from the helmet to make the blonde woman strong. Sometimes, Gorzo wonders if Doctor Miloff truly believes the special electrons and atoms will make anyone strong or if Doctor Miloff only likes to be cruel.

Cruel, Gorzo believes. Cruel, like those from the orphanage.

Gorzo believes some people like to be cruel. Gorzo no longer believes that Doctor Miloff cares about making anyone strong.

Gorzo did not think before grabbing Doctor Miloff when Doctor Miloff tried to pull the switch down after putting the helmet on the blonde woman. Doctor Miloff slapped Gorzo, but Gorzo ignored the slap. Doctor Miloff reached for his whip, but Gorzo pulled him away from where it hung from the wall. Gorzo dragged Doctor Miloff past the table where the screaming blonde woman lay strapped down.

Gorzo stared at the woman when Gorzo and Doctor Miloff passed her. Gorzo knew the look in her eye. Gorzo felt how she felt when Gorzo lived in the orphanage. If Gorzo could speak, he knew to say nothing.

Gorzo dragged Doctor Miloff across the room, past the machine with the wire, beyond the lab door, and down the hall.

To the trap door.

Gorzo was strong enough to hold Doctor Miloff under one arm and open the trap door with the other. Gorzo looked at Doctor Miloff and saw the fear on his face. The nerve of Doctor Miloff.

Gorzo dropped Doctor Miloff down the trap door to the watery basement below. Doctor Miloff was never Gorzo's friend. Gorzo's pet was never his friend. Let Doctor Miloff and Gorzo's pet be friends.

Gorzo would soon free the blonde-haired woman from her table. Gorzo knew once she was free, she would run. She'd tell others what happened, and they'd come to Gorzo's home.

Doctor Miloff's home. Doctor Miloff's old home.

Gorzo can no longer stay here. Gorzo did not know where to go. Gorzo would be alone in the world again.

For the first time in a long time, Gorzo felt happy.

Swing and a Miss

"Why did you come here?"

"I'm a drunk."

"When do you plan on leaving?"

"When I'm drunk."

"You're already drunk."

"I think I'll stay."

That's how Paul and the bartender's conversation went. That's how the conversations between Paul and the bartender always went. They don't converse much when they talk because neither talks much.

Not that Paul felt averse to conversations. It's that the bartender and the world felt averse to conversing with Paul.

Paul liked to rest his head on his hand and bent elbow when he sat at the bar. He looked bored when he struck the pose, but he wasn't bored. Paul used the head-and-elbow gimmick as a way to look bored so people would talk to him.

Paul desperately needed a new gimmick.

A guy sat beside Paul to his right, looking down at the horse race results on his tablet. A young lady sat to Paul's left with her back turned to him. If someone sat on the lady's other side, she'd be in a perfect position for a conversation. She faced an empty chair, facing this way to avoid any encouragement from Paul about starting a conversation.

Paul felt bored for real.

His mind went blank as he lifted a lime margarita from its temporary resting place on the bar. Paul pressed his thumb down on the stirring straw inside the margarita glass. He pressed the straw against the glass for no reason but to scratch at the salt on the rim. Pressing on the straw and rim gave him something to do.

Paul looked around the half-empty bar. A few people were having fun laughing and joking with each other. Paul didn't enter—never entered—the bar with anyone else. He sat at the bar solo, sipping his margarita before placing it back on top of the water ring the glass left on the bar's countertop.

Paul reached into his pocket. Time to do what all the lonely people do in this place: pull out the smartphone. He became uninspired immediately after unlocking the device, so he put the phone and its cracked screen next to the margarita on the bar.

Tired of looking at everyone sitting around the place, Paul's eyes drifted above the bar to the LED television playing a baseball game. Paul didn't even know the team names anymore. After getting cut from his high school team, he stopped watching baseball. God, he was a big baseball fan back in the old times. Paul knew all the teams, the top players, who won, who lost, and who won or lost what championship in what year.

Today, he only distinguished the two teams playing as "red" and "blue."

One team is on the field while the other goes to bat a single player at a time. Paul remembered stuff like that.

He didn't remember where that gambling app was on his smartphone screen. Paul scrolled from the first screen to the last. Where's that app?

Paul's eyes glanced away from the smartphone to the baseball game. He caught a swing-and-a-miss at its tail end.

Eyes go right back to the smartphone screen. Fingers move a bit slower because Paul wasn't sold on gambling apps. Paul barely knew how to use the aging smartphone, much less the apps he had little use for. The gambling app grabbed his attention, so he downloaded it. Although Paul stopped following sports years ago, he figured making an educated guess on a wager might put some money in his pocket.

While in dire need of some cash, Paul wasn't foolish enough to risk anything by gambling. Adding gambling losses to his scorecard stood among the bottom rung of things he needed to accomplish.

Paul's eyes darted from the smartphone screen to the television, back to the smartphone screen, back to the television, and to the smartphone screen, back to the television.

Paul only broke the rhythm when he heard the bar's front door swing open, and some guy dressed in out-of-style clothes walked inside. Paul immediately lost interest in the guy before ever feeling any initial interest.

Paul tapped the gambling app, logged on, and saw he could still get some action on the game, even though it already started. The online casino app gave Paul a chance to troll for a conversation.

"Hey, you know you can bet pitch-by-pitch with this thing?" Paul blurted what he saw on the app's display out loud, hoping he'd draw in a conversation.

The guy on Paul's right and the lady on Paul's left ignored him. The bartender acknowledged the comment with a "Yeah." The word intended to preserve capitalism through not dissuading Paul from buying more drinks and leaving a tip.

Paul's eyes returned to the gambling app, and he pondered placing a bet on a random pitch, hoping to kill some boredom.

What else could he do in the bar besides watch the "reds" and "blues" play?

He'd soon start watching the guy with the out-of-date clothes who walked inside.

Who is this odd guy? Paul soon received an answer - but no penny - for his thought.

P.K. Nadelstern
Fortune Telling. Divination. Life Coach.

Those were the only words on P.K. Nadelstern's business card. The image of something - crossed swords? - sat centered between the words, but Paul deduced they existed to take up space. He heard the words "take up space" all through elementary school and liked using the line long past graduation.

Paul learned enough in elementary school to deduce Nadelstern wore out-of-date clothes because the fortune-telling hustle did little more than make Nadelstern a preferred VIP shopper at all the local thrift stores.

Or was he one of those wildly successful hustlers who liked being a cheapskate?

Paul glanced at the business card for a second. He started to stare for longer than a second as his thoughts drifted. They drifted because Paul downed three margaritas and now switched to a light beer with a mere 4% alcohol content. The 4% read a postscript to the higher percentage drinks he previously consumed.

"Huckleman's coming up next," P.K. Nadelstern mentioned to Paul, who never heard of Huckleman. Paul's eyes drifted back to the LED television above the bar, watching the reds and the blues continue their baseball game.

"Huckleman's a first baseman or something?" Paul asked Nadelstern.

"He's a something. He's a catcher." Nadelstern smiled, deflecting from his baseball hipness.

"You know he's coming up to bat because you're a fortune teller? That's supposed to sell me on what you're selling?" Paul struck a defensive posture, not wanting to look too willing to speak to the man everyone else in the bar ignored.

"I know Huckleman's coming up to bat because he follows Edlemile in the lineup."

"Fortune telling tell you that?"

"No. I'm a baseball fan."

Paul sunk into the barstool. He heard some snickers from patrons overhearing the conversation. Paul wanted to give the snickerers dirty looks. He never did.

"I can see the live updates on your phone." Nadelstern nodded his head slightly at the smartphone on the bar. Paul wanted to slap himself. He had forgotten he had put the phone on the bar, where a slickster like Nadelstern could swipe it without Paul noticing.

Paul's eyes focused on the smartphone's screen. Alcohol-blurred vision didn't reach the point where he couldn't make up the wagering info on the screen.

"You know you can bet on each pitch?" Nadelstern pointed out.

"I know. I've been thinking about it," Paul admitted. "I feel I don't need to know much about the players when betting on a pitch. Dumb luck's all you need."

"Thinking won't put money in your pocket. You have to wager." Nadelstern spoke a half-truth. You had to win the bet to collect anything.

Nadelstern's words made sense but reminded Paul of a looming hustle. Nadelstern tried handing his business card to every other patron and clown in the bar, but they all blew him off. If he didn't order a drink soon, the bartender would probably throw him out. The bartender knew that Paul would be dumb enough to buy the hustler a drink, so he didn't push Nadelstern out the door too quickly.

Poor Paul. He grew a bit tired of looking like a mark. What irked Paul the most was that everyone in the bar thought of him that way. No eyes rested on him, but he felt the attitude linger in the air.

"You know what Huckleman's going to do at bat, right?" Paul asked with a stern voice.

"I have an idea. A vision."

"All I have to do is buy you a drink, right? You'll reveal all, right?" Paul started getting hostile. Boredom caused him to let his guard down with Nadelstern, and he began to feel the embarrassment of his behavior. Raising his voice had a last-ditch element to it. Paul hoped changing his pitch would change how the disinterested bar patrons perceived him. Raising his voice did little more than swing and miss.

"All you need to do is place the bet and give me a fair tip if you win." Nadelstern's terms seem reasonable.

"Right." Paul turned his head away from Nadelstern, bringing the beer glass to his lips as he watched the replay of ball four and a player getting a walk to first base.

"Wouldn't hurt to try." Nadelstern seemed pushy but didn't ask Paul to do anything that benefitted the seeming hustler.

"How much am I supposed to sink on the bet?" Paul wondered.

"Whatever you want."

"I want you to go hustle someone else." Paul felt self-conscious about looking like a fool. The smart comment sought to elicit a preferred response from the bar patrons. None came.

"Huckleman's coming up to bat soon."

Paul grabbed the smartphone off the bar and recklessly tapped on the screen. "Here you go, here you go," Paul snapped as he played with the wagering app.

"Oh, you should wait a second!" Nadelstern tried to admonish Paul.

"Too late," Paul revealed. "I put a ten spot on Huckleman getting a hit on the third pitch. Pays 40 to 1."

"Shame. That app allows you to get much more specific on the pitch wagers. Your batter is going to hit a double on the third pitch. Wagering on that outcome pays 140 to 1." Strange how Nadelstern knew the odds.

Paul didn't care. Everything he did served to set up proving Nadelstern was a hustler, and Paul could show the world (aka bar patrons) nobody could sucker him. That'd be his grand accomplishment for the day and week.

Paul said nothing to Nadelstern. He just folded his arms as he watched Huckleman up at bat.

Swing and a miss on the first pitch. Swing and a miss on the second pitch. Pine connects with the ball on the third swing, and the ball flies into the outfield, bouncing between center and left field. By the time the left-fielder caught the ball, Huckleman had made his way to second base.

Paul sat there looking dumbfounded. Nadelstern broke the silence, telling Paul, "Next time. Wait until I tell you what wager to place."

The bar patrons did pay attention to the show. Paul knew they did because he could hear their snickers.

———— ◉ ————

A COUPLE OF DAYS PASSED.

The margarita was gone before Paul even noticed he downed it. The bartender noticed. That's why he came over to nudge Paul with two curt words, "Want another?"

Paul looked up at him and almost gave a wiseass answer, saying, "Want, yes? Need? No." Paul figured wising off to the bartender came with no upsides. He still didn't feel like talking much. Paul nodded without looking at the bartender. He nodded and motioned, "Gimme, gimme," with his hands.

Paul tried to make it seem like he didn't look up because he was busy doing something important. Truth is (and "was" and "will be") Paul's broke. He's also busy and doing something important. Paul checked the balance on his one credit card that didn't hit the maxed-out point. Lucky Paul. He had $83 left on the card before hitting the ceiling. If Paul put the $17 in his pocket toward his bar bill and charged the rest, he'd have $58 to last until tomorrow. What he'd do after tomorrow, Paul didn't know.

For now, Paul could have one more margarita and watch the end of the baseball game. A green team is playing a yellow team tonight. Two innings left, and still no Nadelstern.

Paul couldn't determine Nadelstern's angle. The guy didn't hit him up for any money (yet), so being a no-show served no purpose other than making Paul look like a dope.

Lots of folks liked making Paul look like a dope. "Fellas think stuff like that's funny," Paul thought to himself as the bartender put the margarita down on the bar. Partners and associates made a dope out of him in enough business opportunities to drive Paul to the edge of bankruptcy. Not keeping up with changes in technology helped high-risk financial arrows pierce Paul's entrepreneurial armor. Don't expect him to admit such shortcomings.

Swing and a miss. The yellow team's last batter struck out, and the game headed into the final inning. Paul planned on downing his last margarita before heading home. He would only worry about how to deal with tomorrow once it came. When it arrived, Paul planned to worry a lot.

Paul jumped when he felt a hand on his shoulder. "Why so nervous?" were the words Paul heard behind him. He turned to see the guest he'd been expecting since the third inning. Nadelstern.

"Any good reason why you're late?" Paul asked as the TV over the bar went from commercial to back to the game. The yellow team would soon take its chance at bat.

"I can predict many things and change nothing," Nadelstern replied. "I can predict heavy traffic during rush hour, but I can't change it."

"Yeah," Paul slurred. "I know how you feel. I can't change much of anything, either."

Nadelstern's eyes drifted to the smartphone on the bar, then shifted to the baseball game playing on the television. He didn't notice Paul had reflexively grabbed the phone off the bar. The last thing Paul needed was someone stealing a four-year-old, failing smartphone. Four years old and failing, notwithstanding, Paul lacked the cash and credit to replace it. At least the phone still works for now.

"Since we only have an inning left, you want to get to business?" Paul had zero interest in pleasantries, and it wasn't the alcohol talking.

"Bledom. Third pitch. Foul ball," Nadelstern responded without letting a single breath delay him. He added, "80 to one odds and payout."

Paul ran the math through his head. He's great with running math. It's a skill Paul learned from constantly looking at unpayable bills and trying to scheme a way to cover the debts. Scheming's all he could do. It's not like he could pay any creditors with a non-existent honest income.

The math on this one only required the calculator on Paul's smartphone - not that he needed it. 80 x $50 paid $4,000. He could pay off a credit card with a win. "A" credit card - singular.

"If that's the best bet I'm going to get, I'll go with it," Paul said to Nadelstern, although Paul was really talking to himself.

"It's not the best bet. It's the least risky," Nadelstern's words sounded like a disclaimer.

"Now you're saying the plays don't always work out the way you say. Figures." Paul couldn't hide his cynicism.

"The bet will win. That's not where the risk is," Nadelstern noted cryptically.

"So what's the best bet?" Paul wanted to know.

"I don't think you're the type who gels well with high risk," Nadelstern responded.

"Just give me the bet that pays the biggest," pushed Paul. He heard that one guy in the back of the bar snickering.

"I'm not sure the risk is worth the trouble," Nadelsterm commented, trying to discourage Paul.

"JUST GIVE ME THE BEST BET!" Paul's voice boomed, and everyone in the bar looked in his direction. Paul had long passed the point of feeling embarrassed.

Nadelstern gave Paul what he wanted. "Bledom. Fourth pitch. Pop up. The third baseman catches it."

Paul didn't even look in Nadelstern's direction. He plugged a $50 bet into the smartphone. The 400 to 1 payout on a $50 bet meant $20,000.

Paul entered the bet into his smartphone just in time. The yellow pitched the ball to the batter, Beldom. Swing. Hit. Pop-up in the direction of third base. Too bad for Beldom. The third baseman caught the ball. Good for Paul. He's $20,000 richer now.

Time stopped for Paul. When it dawned on him that he'd won the crazy bet, he jumped up from the barstool in joy. Shame he didn't clear that barstool. It caught his foot, and Paul fell straight to the ground, twisting his ankle on the fall. Paul could hear the pop before he hit the ground.

The pain shot up Paul's leg and hit his brain as he suffered an ankle sprain. Paul's pride joined his ankle in ill feelings when the bar's snickers expanded beyond the earlier solo act.

Paul rubbed his leg as he looked up at Nadelstern. The fortune teller had terse words for the winner, "Like I said, some bets come with greater risks."

<hr>

NADELSTERN'S LOOK TOLD the story when Paul handed him $2,000, a 10% tip. Paul figured that Nadelstern got a fair cut, although Nadelstern disagreed. He didn't argue with Paul. Nadelstern knew customers paid what they'd pay.

Nadelstern appreciated the 10% enough to show up at the bar on Sunday. Sunday stood as the agreed-upon meeting for his next endeavor with Paul. Paul sat at the same barstool, drinking his margarita and eating pork chops, mixed vegetables, and coleslaw.

Paul had never ordered food before because he couldn't afford it. He could do so now, thanks to the $20,000 the online casino deposited into his account.

No, Paul didn't pay off any credit cards with the $20,000 he received. Sure, he planned on paying off his cards, but that could wait until mid-week. By the end of Sunday evening, Paul knew - or believed - he wouldn't struggle again.

Paul didn't even care why Nadelsterm didn't use his powers of predictions to place his own bets. At least he didn't care before finally asking Nadelstern, "Why don't you place bets for yourself if you know so much?"

Nadelstern replied, "Fortune tellers can see other people's futures, not their own."

"You don't know what the future holds for our little arrangement?" Paul asked.

"I have a good idea," Nadelstern responded.

Paul picked up on the backhanded insult but didn't say anything that would irk the man helping to put money in his pocket. Instead, Paul chose to ask the non-million-dollar question. "Why didn't you push me to make a bigger bet if you knew it'd win?"

"Because you'd win," Nadelstern noted.

"Say what?" Paul couldn't determine why Nadelstern would bogart how much Paul could win. Why would he cheat himself out of a generous tip? Was Nadelstern planning on some kind of sly con job?

"Winning is what the game's about, right?" Paul had a point.

"Not if you're the bank." Nadelstern had a point.

"What would they care? 99% of the characters placing those bets lose. Why would a casino app's management care about one or two big payoffs?" Paul needed a fortune teller to give him the answer because he never saw the whole picture.

"Casinos, like all businesses, don't like to pay. They start taking notice of people who win big with longshot bets." Nadelstern let his response hang in the bar's stale air a bit before adding, "If they think somebody's scheming them, expect someone to come knocking."

"That's what your fortune-telling skills tell you?"

"No. Experience tells me." Nadelstern loved to let words hang in stale air, so he waited a second before asking Paul, "What's prudence telling you?"

"Who's she?"

"Who's who?"

"Prudence."

"No. Small 'p.' No capitals or proper names."

"Say what again?"

Nadelstern finished his glass of non-alcoholic soda water, using the time to keep his composure and think about explaining things to Paul in the simplest of terms.

"I'd suggest you take two weeks off and then make a reasonable bet." Nadelstern hoped Paul would take his advice.

"Aren't you in business to make money?" Paul wondered with an accusatory tone.

"Yes," Nadelstern replied. "That's why I have to run to see some other customers."

"I want to make a big bet. $10,000 on something that pays big. Can you do that?" Paul.

"Not really."

"Come on!" came the agitated response from Paul. "You playing games? Won't you give me something that'll pay off big?"

Paul ducked his head slightly after his slight outburst as the bar's denizens again took notice of his odd behavior.

Nadelstern took a turn at feeling agitated, but he had a passive way of expressing his emotions. Not that he hid the agitated tone in his voice. "I can give you half of what you want and half of what you absolutely don't want."

"Say what one more time?"

"I can help you with a winning bet. That's the first half," Nadelstern said, adding, "The other half would be the consequences that come with it. Can't help you there."

"Why do you care?" Paul sincerely wanted an answer.

"I run honest entrepreneurial endeavors," Nadelsterm replied, adding, "Reputation counts for everything. A good fortune teller with a good reputation is an honest fortune teller, an aberration.

Nadelstern turned to Paul, adding, "Far too many schemers and connivers in the fortune-telling game."

Paul shook his head in disbelief. Not about the fortune telling that put some hard (un)earned gambling winnings in his pocket. Cash in the pocket can make someone a believer in the craziest things. Paul couldn't believe such an easy deal could ever go south.

"What consequences am I going to run into other than not knowing how to spend all that money?"

Nadelstern responded with a question that double-served as good advice. "Have you thought of saving what you win? Long-term investments could work out better."

"I don't get you sometimes."

"No, you don't," Nadelstern acknowledged before adding, "You don't know the risks of drawing attention to yourself. As someone who runs an honest business, I want to keep you in good standing - karma and all. You know, what goes around comes around, right?"

"Right."

"I think it's best to drop off someone's radar before getting on. Lose some bets. Lose a few random bets. Wait a couple weeks. Win one last time and then lose a few more. Let the world chalk the wins up to luck."

"As opposed to doing what?"

"Proving how smart you are. Trust my experience. I predict no one cares."

Paul bit his tongue for a second, not wanting to get on the bad side of the one guy who did him some good. Paul took a pause by looking up at the television screens and watching the sports analysts talk. The sound was off, and Paul didn't read lips. He didn't look at the closed captioning. Why bother? Since when did an analyst give him insight worth anything?

Paul snapped back into the moment.

"C'mon, what's so hard about the whole deal? I place 20 bets at a thousand bucks each with 20 different casinos." Paul spoke with sincerity, not seeing the big picture.

"We're not doing 20 bets, friend."

"Great, we'll pick one grand slam pitch or close to it."

"No. Too....grand."

"What do you care? Since when is fortune telling illegal?"

Nadelstern took his turn at a rare display of drawing attention. The nominally disinterested (although still occasionally eavesdropping) hangers-on in the bar glanced in the fortune teller's direction when he couldn't hold in his scoffing.

"You'll care when you have other concerning things to worry about. You don't think someone will show up wondering how you keep winning big on off-the-wall bets?"

"What would some 20-year-old tech nerd care?" Paul liked asking questions that sought to sell his daydreams.

"A 20-year-old tech nerd might develop the app, but the business the apps associated with isn't run by a 20-year-old or a nerd."

"You get a vision about a big crime syndicate hiding out the other end of a smartphone speaker?"

"I have a vision for running a low-key business," Nadelstern responded. "I am also ethical and humane enough to worry about consequences."

"Oh, c'mon, please." Paul had a weary cynicism that prompted his further agitated comment. Jonesing for more cash is what agitated him further.

"One more bet. I won't walk out on you. I led you here and didn't want to make any bad karma for myself by leading people on and then leaving them hanging."

"Or lose somebody else's future business," said St. Paul the Cynical.

"...I am telling you now, in advance, you get one more bet. Then, we're done."

"How about something 200 to 1?"

"No. No way. No chance. No how." Nadelstern nodded "No" with his head to drive the point home.

"C'mon." Paul tried to nudge Nadelstern.

"No," Nadelstern said unnudged.

Paul sighed in displeasure, and Nadelstern clarified things. "One last bet, friend. Decent payout. I'll go for that."

"A decent payout could be enough to make me eat the finest of food. On Sundays." Paul smiled, counting the imaginary winnings in his head.

"I'm capping your bets." Nadelstern refused to nudge and budge.

"What?"

"That's it, friend. Enough. You could walk away with another generous sum. Invest it wisely because we're done after that."

"I still will owe you $1,000, right?"

"Up to you."

"No payment upfront?"

"No."

"You trust me?" Paul didn't ask the question to be a wise guy. He sincerely wasn't used to meeting trusting people.

"Yes, I'm the trusting type. Too trusting. I trust you to use your head and do the right thing."

One old phrase could give both Paul and Nadelstern better advice. Don't bet on it.

———⊙———

BARRO, THE CENTERFIELDER, walked up to the plate. His uniform looked exceptionally bright on the high-definition television hanging over the bar.

"Imagine if Barro hit an inside-the-park home run. Imagine what a dollar bet on that one would pay out. Imagine if you bet a dollar on Barro hitting an inside-the-park homerun on the third pitch. The payout could buy you a house in Hawaii." Paul liked to spend money he hadn't yet won.

"The payout would buy you Hawaii." Nadelstern made a rare funny. After the one-sentence funny, the fortune teller returned to his typical dryness. "The chances of anyone hitting an inside-the-park homerun throughout their entire career would be a million-to-one."

"A guy can dream, they say. Now, I'm going to say I want a bet that pays 1,000 to one."

"No." Nadelstern had an emphatic inflection that drove the two-letter word home.

"Come on."

"No." Nadelstern barely moved his head. "This will be the last bet we do. It's the last fortune I tell you."

"Any reason why?" Paul could understand why anyone would walk away from a sure bet and a big payoff.

"Greed isn't good for your health," Nadelstern said the words in a way that hinted he worried about his own well-being. He didn't need fortune-telling skills to know guys like Paul can get you into trouble. They can make you a few bucks, but keep them as short-timers.

"How much fortune are you going to bestow upon me?" Paul never took his eyes off Barro and the television screen. That's not all true. Paul's eyes would glance at his smartphone positioned by his margarita. Paul always worried about somebody stealing his smartphone from the bar. Happened before.

"I'll think a bit and give you something that pays 100 to 1."

"I can make a lot with a 100 to 1. They'll cap me at a $1,000 bet - casino rules - but $100,000 payout...."

"$10,000."

"I wish they'd let me bet $10,000."

"I mean, I'm only helping you win $10,000 by placing a $100 bet."

"Say what?" Paul asked the reflexive question with shock. $10,000 would be half of what he won the last time.

"$10,000," Nadelstern reiterated. "You'll win the $10,000 all nice, safe, and random. Place five $100 bets in a row and walk away a happy winner on bet five. $10,000 richer. No one will notice."

Nadelstern checked out what was happening on the monitor. Why is the umpire holding up the game? Nadelstern took the delay to add, "People notice when they have to pay out $10,000, but they'll chalk it up to random luck if it looks that way. You add a zero, people will want to know why you got so lucky so often." Nadelstern didn't take his eyes off the television screen when he suggested, "These things play out safer when they look random."

Paul looked around the nearly empty bar to see if anyone picked up on their conversation. No one cared. "My man, what are you doing to me here?"

"Keeping you from being noticed and helping to put money in your pocket."

From the corner of his eye, Paul noticed the lady who sat next to him and had ignored him a week or so before. She was leaning her ear oddly, now pretending not to notice him.

The game's back on, and Barro's ready for the first pitch. Paul and Nadelstern stopped talking to watch the game. Nadelstern had nothing to add, and Paul didn't know what to say. Why not watch the game?

Barro took a swing and hit a foul ball. Paul never understood why Barro always swung on the first pitch. With the next pitch, Barro didn't swing - he never swung on the second pitch - and he lucked out because this pitch ended up being ball one.

Nadelstern said the words that drew Paul's eyes and ears away from the ballgame. "Start making the $100 bets."

"What swing am I betting on? What's the batter going to do? What's going to be the payoff?" Paul's erratic questioning revealed he wanted to speed up fame and fortune - more so fortune.

"Start making the $100 bets. Bet whatever comes to your head on each pitch. Won't matter. You'll pick losers before I tell you a winner."

Paul punched a $100 bet on his smartphone. The casino took the credits from the deposits in his account, which were in the $3,000 range.

Paul didn't even think about what he was betting, so he bet on a swing and a miss with the next pitch. Barro didn't swing at all. Strike two.

"Barro's running out of chances here.' Paul tried to nudge Nadelstern, who didn't nudge. Paul lost another $100 on the next bet. He bet a 10,000-to-one shot, a triple on the pitch. Barro hit a foul ball that went into the stands, giving a lucky fan a souvenir. Paul found himself down another $100. Two more foul balls left him another $200 poorer.

Paul began to feel like Nadelstern was playing a gag on him until the vaunted fortune teller said, "Bet on a double." That's a 100-to-1 bet. Paul's pre-planned and self-inflicted losing streak made him a little leery, but he knew he had to get the bet in quickly before the next pitch.

Drawing on his unsuccessful entrepreneurial background, Paul knew Nadelsterm wouldn't feed him a loser at crunch time, or else he'd risk his customer taking a walk, bringing his tip with him. Paul had no guarantees what Nadelstern planned for the next bet, but Paul thought now was a great time to make a real wager.

Nadelstern enjoyed a rare adult beverage, so he didn't catch Paul's finger actions on the smartphone after Paul hit the "enter" on the bet. *A $1,000 bet.*

Nadelstern's eyes bugged when Paul put $1,000 on the pitch. The fortune teller felt so shocked at Paul's double-cross that he froze. The pitcher's pitch didn't freeze. It traveled from the mound to Barro, the batter.

Everything moved quickly. Swing. Hit. Fly ball. The center fielder runs after it and doesn't catch it. The ball bounces. And bounces. The ball ends up in the left fielder's glove. The left fielder throws it to second base. He throws it to second base because he has to go through the motions. Barro easily makes it to second, safe.

Nadelstern glares at Paul who smirks. Why wouldn't he smirk? He's $100,000 richer.

Paul tuned Nadelstern out and jumped off his bar stool, screaming, "That's the grand slam, folks! The grand slam!"

Everyone looked at Paul dumbfounded. They had no idea what made him animated, and they didn't care enough about him to ask.

"Enjoy your drinks, folks!" Paul exclaimed. "I thought for a second of buying everyone in the place a round."

The promise of free drinks got everyone's attention, and Paul capitalized on the attention by saying, "Then I said, 'Why would I associate with losers?'"

———— ◦ ————

TWO DAYS WENT BY BEFORE Paul returned to the bar. Paul took his seat at his personally famous bar, an establishment across the street from his bank. Paul waited two business days before returning to the because that's how long it takes for the wire transfer to deposit his $100,000. Today would be his last day in the bar because a $100,00 richer Paul had zero intentions about coming back and hanging with the losers.

The casino app credited his account right away, and Paul felt so joyous about getting the money that he didn't care that the bank would report it as taxable. They will when the deposit arrives in a half hour, the expected delivery time.

Aww, hell, who cares about the taxes? Give the IRS whatever the hell it wants. Be happy with the found money that found you.

Paul had thoughts like that. He also felt generous - and lousy. He double-crossed Nadelstern and committed to giving the man a $25,000 tip. Less if Nadelstern keeps him waiting longer. There's nary a Nadelstern in the bar. You'd think the man would show up to collect his payoff.

Hate me all you want, but don't you love the money? Those are the kind of thoughts that run through the mind of a guy like Paul.

Paul sipped at his Margarita, his second Margarita. Paul had little interest in drinking a third, so his fortune-telling benefactor had until the last salty sip to pick up a tip.

A tap on the shoulder prompted thoughts in Paul's head. *Nadelstern. I knew he'd come around to say his goodbyes and collect a cut.*

Paul turned to say hello to Nadelstern but would have to settle for saying hello to three strangers. Three big strangers. In suits.

"Come on, time to talk." The words came from the big fellow standing between two bigger dudes.

Paul should have remembered gambling apps require a photo identification when opening an account. Photo identifications display addresses.

Addresses. Neighbors. Landlords. People who knew a tenant's habits.

Thoughts like that bunted Paul's other thoughts about how he'd spend his money into foul ball territory.

"I guess I'm easy to find," Paul said as one of the bigger guys grabbed his arm and pulled him from his bar seat.

"Guys," Paul spoke to buy time, hoping the bartender would call the cops. Yeah, right. Paul continued. "We don't need any trouble."

"There won't be any trouble," the big guy in the middle said. "As long as you can show us how you're the only lug on this big blue marble called Earth who can pull off those crazy bets."

Paul took that as his cue to run. He got half a step before a fist hit him hard in the gut.

The bartender pretended not to notice. He didn't need to prove not to care.

Paul's knees hit the floor hard, and he gasped for air. The pain in his gut from the punch lingered. While the shot dropped him and clouded his mind, it didn't send for a big enough loop to know sticking around the bar was a bad idea. Paul rose halfway from the ground and sprinted to the door. He relied on the skills he had when he tried out for the track team in High School.

One of the thugs who waltzed into the bar relied on a beer bottle he grabbed off the counter to smash Paul back into a more compliant state.

The bottle shattered when it hit Paul, sending him to the ground again while also relaying reminders he didn't make the track team in High School.

Paul's knees hit the ground again, and his spinning head could barely make out the words the thugs were saying.

"$100. $100. $100. $1000? Lose. Lose. Lose. Win? Who you kidding?"

They dragged Paul out the door with plans to take him to parts unknown. Paul got hit so hard his head drooped all the way out the door.

"Somehow, we are going to find out how you became the smartest lug on the whole big blue marble."

Paul raised his head once as the three-man riot squad dragged him to a luxury car parked in front of the bar. Paul heard their words but barely registered them.

"We got a gorgeous television. I don't know how many inches of screen it's got, like I don't know how you make and win them bets."

When Paul raised his head, he saw an expressionless Nadelstern standing by the front door. The fortune teller finally arrived.

"We got two TVs, and there's two games on tonight. Let's see how you make them freak-o bets."

Paul let his head drop down once more. Why ask for help when none will come?

All Paul could do as he found himself thrown in the luxury car's backseat involved practicing self-fortune telling, and the immediate future looked bleak.

Paul thought about the money and knew why they cut him from his high school team. *I hit a grand slam and still swung and missed.*

The Menace of the Mansion

The 1928 Dietrich Limousine had little trouble heading up the paved road on the hill. The hill wasn't steep, and the limo appeared well-maintained for a model that's been in use for the past six years. The owner would never send an unimpressive car to pick up guests. Llewellyn Creighton always took care of the things he owned. The big house on top of the steep hill with the winding, winding road stood as a testament to how much pride Creighton took in his possessions.

"Why wouldn't he? It's all he has in the world anymore, right?" Robert asked the question with his typical lack of class. The limo's chauffeur ignored him, keeping his eye on the road.

"I don't think he wants anything else. Or needs anything else," Mayra mused from her passenger seat. The chauffeur continued to say nothing, keeping his hands on the oversized wheel and his eyes on the narrow road.

"Hey," Conrad directed the comment to the chauffeur. Is it true that old L.C. doesn't speak anymore? He stopped talking out of some protest about the business going from silent movies to talkies?" The chauffeur didn't appear to be a fan of talkies, as he wouldn't talk.

"I hear he likes the silent types. He pays gophers and other mugs to keep quiet. Life's a big silent movie for an old star who won't talk." Robert had to get his unsolicited opinions into the mix.

"He doesn't speak because he can't speak," Mayra let the words slip from her tongue with condescension. Shouldn't they know about Mr. Creighton's newspaper-rumored plight? "Throat cancer is why he won't talk."

"Doesn't need to talk." Conrad had a point.

"Not when he was making silent movies. All he had to do was make those faces." Robert knows so little.

"What great and scary faces they were." Mayra, so correct.

"Shame he picked up the smoking habit. Took all he had in his throat away. Shame. He was such a great theater star before the movies."

"He was greater in the movies."

The comments blended together.

"The war that took his throat also took half his face." Old Sam felt the need to interject, a feeling he had since the trip began. The gruff studio executive found the time arrived to exert control over his underlings. "Losing his face worked out for him with the horror movies. Why wouldn't losing his voice do the same?" Old Sam had that business-oriented attitude. Everyone else in the limo loved the movie business because they fashioned themselves as Bohemian artists, heavily emphasizing the Bohemian.

"You think he's lonely living in that mansion by himself?" Mayra asked, glancing at quiet Anna.

"He doesn't have time to feel lonely," Robert curtly replied. "Old Mr. Creighton's too busy counting his money to feel lonely."

Robert seems to prevent young Anna from getting a chance to reply. At least, that's how observers would see it. Anna doesn't speak, and she hasn't spoken in several years.

"I heard he hasn't said a word since the big mess on the last film."

"He *can't* talk to anyone."

"Who's he going to talk to up on that big house on the big hill?"

Uniformed comments blended again. That's how Anna perceived them, at least.

"He *wouldn't* talk to anyone if he *could* talk to anyone, isn't that right?" The chauffeur didn't respond, which should be unsurprising by now. No one in the limo wanted a response from the chauffeur; they just wanted to get on his nerves. The chauffeur's silent treatment gave no indication of how he felt.

"Old Creighton's the only guy who came out on top when the market crashed. Smart man."

"Too smart for an actor."

"Former actor."

"Soon to be current actor," Sam piped in, "He'll come around."

Anna listened to everyone's banter, noting that everyone sounded more like they were talking to themselves than each other.

"Who'd think the star of **The Menace of the Mansion** would live in a big mansion on a hill like the one in the film?" Robert wondered.

"Who'd think a silent movie would make money on a re-release?" Mayra's musings posed a good question.

"Who'd think little kids would pack a theater on a cheap matinee to see the old film?" Conrad followed up on the good question.

"Doesn't matter what anyone thinks," Sam had to chime in again, being the only person who knew the score. "The ticket sales tell the tale."

"You think you could coax him out of retirement?" Mayra's next good question has a serious undertone.

Sam smirked as he replied, "Do you think he wants to stay a forgotten recluse in an old mansion?" A serious question with no undertone needing interpretation.

Silence became a briefly embraced theme. The only sound was the humming of the limo's engine. The limo struggled on the road on the steep hill, but it kept moving onward to the mansion at the top.

"Old Creighton...." Robert liked to refer to Creighton as "old Creighton" because he found rudeness humorous.

"He's not that old...." Don't expect Mayra to admit she found the former silent star strangely attractive. Everyone knew that's how she felt, but they knew to stay quiet.

"Smoking makes him look older..." Conrad didn't lie.

"Mustard gas burns make him look even older...." Robert loved getting his digs in on the old star.

"Mustard gas burns made him a great horror star." Mayra tried to find the good side of a terrible situation.

"Silent movie horror star. They don't make silent movies anymore." Robert stays consistent.

"Monsters and madmen don't have to talk." Mayra kept making sense.

"Temperamental actors who don't need the money don't have to do anything they don't want to do." Sam has a point. "He'll come around," Sam said with confidence. "It's been seven years since *The Menace of the Mansion*. That was his biggest hit, and he had a lot of hits. He has to miss those days." Sam's words brought a silent pause for thought to the limo's interior. Briefly.

The limo continued its journey up the hill as the silence ended and the prattle carried forth. Anna's head remained still, but her eyes darted to the sources of the rampant comments.

"He can't talk."

"He doesn't have to talk."

"He just has to look scary."

"What makes you think he's interested?"

"If he wasn't interested," Sam said with his trademark condescension, "He'd never invite us to his Halloween party."

"He invited us after we *inquired.*"

Sam shot a brutal look that cut off that comment, bringing silence to the limo's interior - albeit brief.

"The whole idea with the costume party is so strange. No one's allowed to speak."

"He was a silent movie star."

"He's a loon."

"He lost his mind on *The Menace of the Mansion.*"

The prattle motivated Anna to interject by raising her two hands and the thumbs and index fingers to make a "W." Everyone got the meaning, so they all glared at her. The glares would strike a remarkable presence if they appeared in a silent movie.

"He lost his wife during *The Menace of the Mansion.*" Mayra took Anna's cue to say the thing no one else wanted to say out loud."

No one wants to talk about the horrible accident that happened during the filming of *The Menace of the Mansion*. They only wanted to talk about how long its ticket lines were.

"For a cursed production, it's been blessed with money-making abilities."

"Keeps making money. Who figured all those little kids would pay money for a re-release of a film where no one talks?"

"Everyone talks. You just can't hear them."

"They might as well not talk."

"The little kids won't care. What else are they going to do at 10 AM on a Saturday?"

"You think old Creighton can still make us money if he plays a monster menace in a new movie?"

The limousine made one last turn on the final winding road at the top of the hill. The mansion loomed not far off in the distance. The chauffeur said nothing, ignoring the braying inside the vehicle. The occupants sounded like rude ticket buyers who couldn't shut up during a movie.

"You think it will stand better than the mansion in the movie?"

"The mansion in the movie wasn't a real mansion."

"It was just a big prop."

"A poorly made prop. A decent mansion prop won't just collapse."

"And if it did, it couldn't kill his wife. She's already dead." Robert chuckled at his observation.

In no world, silent or talkie, was that attempt at humor funny.

"Please be happy guests," Sam suggested in a way that was more than a suggestion. "We need old Creighton back for one more film."

⸻ ● ⸻

LIMOS ARRIVE. GATES open. Visitors enter. Late arrivals change into their costumes.

Old Creighton had enough funds to cover the costume costs for his guests. *All his guests.* The old mansion had well over fifty people packed in the main dining hall.

Fifty daft people, for sure. At least, that's what Sam thought. He wasn't alone. His costuming expert, Conrad, script girl, Mayra, and master set designer, Robert, felt the same. They may not have felt the same way Sam did about fitting into a Henry VIII costume, but they weren't wearing any Henry VIII costumes. ***Henry VIII*** (1922) was a non-horror hit for Llewelyn Crieghton. Sam produced it.

Sam's entourage and the other attendees all wore minimalist masks like him. Almost all of them - Robert's mask looked like an oversized metal waste basket. As long as Robert thought it was a wastebasket, not a torture device that preceded Henry VIII, he'd only worry about the ill fit.

Not that the ill-fitting mask didn't torture Robert. The damned things kept sliding around, to his great annoyance.

Young Anna had no issues with attending the party or wearing the costume from that book about the wizard. At nineteen years of age, Anna entered the seventh year of her acting career. She never reached stardom and knew Llewelan Creighton didn't ask for her presence because of any box office status.

Naive as she was, Anna knew she had received an invite to the party because, like her companions, she was present during the disaster on *The Menace of the Mansion*. Anna kept her mouth shut, unlike the others. She hasn't spoken since the day of the disaster on *The Menace of the Mansion*.

Ever the boisterous executive, Sam had no problem speaking his mind. His entourage kept their voices low to a whisper, not wanting to disturb the festivities. Silent festivities.

Those fifty costumed guests stood, drank, danced, and silently mingled.

The theme of the October costume party stressed one thing. *Silence.* Guests had to keep quiet.

Not every guest heeded the rules, although they only talked to themselves. It was no secret which guests chose to speak to themselves as they entered the dining hall.

"How the hell are we supposed to talk to anyone?"

"Don't talk. Convey. Like a silent movie."

"They don't make silent movies anymore."

"Doesn't mean people can't relive the past."

"Who'd want to relive what happened on *The Menace of the Mansion*?"

"Apparently, the Menace of the Mansion himself. This damn party is right out of the film's second act."

Anna said nothing, as expected. The entourage didn't see how her eyes darted and took all their words in.

"He loved his wife."

"He misses his wife."

"He's a crank."

They joined Anna in silence after running out of breath.

Everyone turned to look at Sam for guidance. The executive whispered heartless comments that came not from the creative wing of the studio but from the accounting department. "All stars are cranks and oddballs, but they make money."

"Silent movies don't make money anymore."

"*The Menace of the Mansion* made money."

"It only made money with kids on a matinee re-release."

"Did it lose money?"

"No."

Finally, silence fell among the entourage that stuck together, not mingling with the other guests. The silence never lasts.

"Why are we here?"

"To make more money."

"How are we going to pitch him on making a new movie if we can't talk?"

"How is he going to make a movie if he can't talk?"

"Won't talk. Not can't talk. I don't buy the cancer story."

"He doesn't have to talk. Creighton can play a silent villain."

The many costumed partygoers continued to dance, and the dancing seemed out of place.

Slow, almost dreaded organ music filled the hall. The dramatic notes mimicked what an audience would hear in a silent movie theater. Audiences didn't appreciate pure silence. Those theaters drifted long ago into memories. Long ago? No, they only stopped making silent movies six years ago. It seemed longer.

Sam deviated from the silent theme one last time when he looked at his entourage and spoke one terse word.

"Mingle."

They moved to mingle, and the silent theme did nothing to distract the question they collectively asked in their heads. What makes someone walk away from money and fame?

Tragic events.

How tragic it was for Llewellyn Creighton to lose his wife on **The Menace of the Mansion.**

What did the newspaper say after the star agreed to finish the film?

You could see the anguish on his face, even underneath the makeup and the mask. The mask hid the makeup, but pulling away the mask showed the makeup couldn't hide the anguish.

Those comments were the gossipy talk that hung over the mystery of Creighton's retirement and self-inflicted exile. Of course, there was no mystery about why he walked away from silent movie fame.

Creighton never once worried about failing to succeed in "talkies," not that such a rumor didn't make the studio and print media rounds.

"When did talking become a must-have for a scary picture to make money? Lots of monsters keep silent. Some only grunt and groan, others growl. Sure, you have ones that like to talk and talk. Kids love them the less the monsters talk."

The out-of-place guests continued their equally out-of-place business-centric conversations, even though the other guests chose to pantomime their conversations in movements. Sam's entourage stood in their ill-fitting costumes off to the side, talking amongst themselves. It didn't matter who said what; they all sang the same spastic song.

"All he needs to do is make two - maybe three - scenes in one of those makeup and costume getups he knows how to put together."

"Would he leave a big house on a big hill to make a movie for little kids?"

"Is he bored enough living in a big house on a big hill to say yes?"

Only Llewellyn Creighton knows the answer, and he's not talking.

"I wonder if he spends time thinking and wonders if Hollywood truly wanted to make silent movies in the first place."

"Or were they placeholders until someone figured out how to deliver sound?"

"Why would Llewellyn Creighton care?"

"He walked away three years before the silent movie era sunsetted."

"He walked away wealthy."

"He walked away without his wife."

"He's lucky he walked away from the disaster."

The "disaster." That's why he walked away from fame. Everyone knew it.

The collective of professionals continued to violate the one rule for the evening: *no talking.* At least they did until other costumed partygoers started glancing in their direction, wondering why the five guests seemed so disinterested and antisocial, hanging together in a highbrow cluster.

"I said, mingle." Sam's words conveyed an order, and Robert, Conrad, Mayra, and quiet Anna followed with what their boss wanted. The group broke apart and moved onto the dance floor, joining the silent festivities.

Saying nothing is easy when you're dancing, and dancing helps buy time as each entourage member tries to deduce how to mingle silently.

The host, Llewellyn Creighton, he'll show up soon. Thoughts ran through their heads as they awaited a host who might not be interested in talking business. Talking business is the only thing the out-of-place guests did, at least until the silent party swallowed them up. That doesn't mean they can't continue to think about business.

Why would he want to start talking on screen? He never spoke on screen before.

He doesn't have to speak if he doesn't want to.

Or he could talk as much as he wants. It's all up to him.

That's how it goes when a studio falls into financial woes and the star doesn't. You can't call Llewellyn Creighton a fallen star. A recluse, yes, but a recluse by choice. ***The Menace of the Mansion*** made money. All of Llewellyn Creighton's films made money.

Sam made a lot of money in the silent movie business. He wants to make more money with sound films. Sam won't use the five-letter word out loud, but he knows he *needs* Llewellyn Creighton to score a new horror hit. Nobody else with a name would work for Sam's now-Poverty Row studio. Creighton would do it for an old friend whose business took a downslide. Sam felt sure.

The out-of-place quartet that accompanied Sam wore awkward-looking costumes. The other anonymous masked guests had well-fitting apparel and period costumes from the 14th century. The evening embraced a medieval theme, although the outfits worn by our five guests matched more contemporary sensibilities.

"Contemporary" didn't refer to 1930's fashion and style. The costume ideas borrowed from clothing in past centuries. Contemporary audiences were familiar with the costumes because they saw them in period-piece films. Did Llewellyn Creighton pilfer the costume department before his limo took him away from the studio the final time?

Conrad looked absurd in a costume that looked like little more than someone wearing a bathrobe with a trash can on their head, an ill-fitting trash can. To Conrad's annoyance, the metal mask was too big for his head and kept sliding around.

"You think somebody could help me with this damn mask? It keeps slipping."

After violating the no-talking rule, Conrad stumbled among the dancing party denizens, and they stared at him. Some turned their heads to lobby funny looks, but they said nothing. No one offered any help.

"Come on," Conrad muttered in a hushed tone. "Somebody has to know how to get this mask to stay straight."

Conrad's other four senses didn't fare much better than his sight, but he recognized the touch that took his hand.

Anna. Like Conrad, she found herself separated from Sam and the others. Anna pulled at Conrad's hand and tried guiding him off to the side, where a marble bench remained affixed to the wall.

Conrad might have better luck fixing things while seated rather than stumbling on the dance floor.

"Thanks, little girl. This cockamamie mask's about to give me a fit." Conrad calmed a bit as Anna led him through a crowd of about fifteen ominously costumed partygoers who all parted to create a path for Anna and her confused companion. More partygoers moved aside to let the two pass until one eerily dressed attendee wouldn't budge. Instead, the odd figure stepped forward between Conrad and Anna, his body cutting through where the two held hands.

The strange guest broke their clasped grip, separating Conrad and Anna. Several partygoers stepped before Anna, blocking her path and vision. Conrad required no assistance with blocked vision, as his poorly fitting mask offered an equally feeble field of view. He couldn't see how the other guests swarmed around him.

The partygoers surrounding Conrad stood still, looking at him in eerie silence.

"I know I'm not supposed to talk, but how about I just don't talk loud?" Conrad threw the line out to the segment of partygoers circling him. "How about someone help me out here?"

Subtlety is the hallmark of a sharp, silent movie performer. Conrad lacked the awareness to pick up on a trained performer's subtleties but noticed something different about the partygoers. They weren't staring at him; they looked over his shoulder.

Conrad never caught the hint that something lurked behind him, so he didn't turn around. The ill-fitting mask would make seeing the eerie attendee standing behind him hard. Conrad might be unable to tell the person was wearing a Black Death-era doctor's costume, the getup with a long, creepy-looking beak.

Neither a clear field of vision nor turning around was necessary to decipher what Conrad felt on his shoulder. The character behind him placed their hand on Conrad.

Conrad broke the rules again, asking the stranger, "Can you help me with this mask, brother? Or is it sister?"

Conrad wouldn't have trouble recognizing the character if he could see out of the damn mask. The iconic costume represented one of the biggest hits and iconic characters of 1920s cinema.

The Menace of the Mansion.

The partygoers formed a semi-circle, although they acted more like an audience watching the Menace of the Mansion perform. The pestilence-protecting costume lived up to its name—the costumed character evoked true menace with his movements behind Conrad.

Conrad remained clueless, unable to see the costumed Menace of the Mansion using exaggerated nimble fingers to tighten the metal waste-basket-like mask sliding atop Conrad's head. The exaggerated nimbleness had an artistic flair, although the meaning seemed missing.

"Thanks, pal," Conrad said too loudly. Saying anything broke the protocol for the party. Saying things loudly seemed overtly rude, but Conrad did things his way and often did things wrong.

Unlike Conrad, the Menace's exaggerations carried meaning. He knew how to draw attention to his fingertips by leaving the rest of his body posture still, like a tremendous silent screen performance.

Conrad mostly ignored the menacing character behind him, thinking only about the mask's annoying ill-fit. Conrad only thought about looking stupid in a mask that kept sliding forward, backward, and side-to-side.

The costumed antagonist kept working his fingers to tighten the mask appropriately. He made one rash action - the Menace of the Mansion yanked his hands away from Conrad exaggeratedly and held his hands up as if to say, "All done."

Conrad took three steps away from his benefactor, bringing his hands to the mask to loosen it. The mask didn't budge. Happy with the fit, Conrad finally turned to see who helped him with the mask.

"Oh, brother," were the only words Conrad could mutter once he came face to face with the Menace of the Mansion. Although he wondered *Has Llewellyn Creighton arrived?* in his head, Conrad could only mumble a two-word refrain of "Oh, brother." The tight-fitting metal mask ceased slipping, making it easier for Conrad to see through the glass-covered eye slits.

Glass-covered?

Conrad realized why he felt so stifled in the mask. Air couldn't come through the eye slits, adding to the mask's stuffiness.

The partygoers couldn't hear the gasp through the metal mask when Conrad backed away from the costumed character. The Menace of the Mansion struck a frightening pose and held his hands in a steeple position, again suggesting, "All done."

Conrad felt uncomfortable in the mask and tried to move it to no avail. He ran his hands across the front of the mask, looking for a latch to open it, as it had become exceptionally uncomfortable. Not only did he find no latch, there were no slits to breathe through the nose or mouth. Tightening the mask cut off the air supply, as there was no space under his chin. The mask clasped tightly to his head.

Conrad turned to the semi-circle of weirdly dressed partygoers who opened the semi-circle so Conrad could have a better path to the dance floor. They had no intention of helping him with the mask. Conrad now picked up on subtleties. Finally.

He could see Mayra and Robert a few yards away through his steaming-up eye slits. The partygoers moved aside to give him a path to his friends, previously hidden by a sea of bodies. Conrad hurried in their direction.

Conrad moved swiftly, panicking - two things that led him to breathe faster.

It took Conrad little time to reach his two friends, now three, who Sam joined. His intuition told him there was trouble on the set. All three broke the party's rules by speaking to Conrad as his panicked movements revealed something wrong. He heard nothing. The airtight mask cut off all sound.

Conrad could barely see through the foggy eye slits. The images Conrad saw before him looked like a movie going out of focus. He did make out Sam, Robert, and Mayra shouting at him in a panic as he fell to the ground.

He fell to the floor, gasping and convulsing.

The crowd of partygoers surrounded Conrad in a quiet circle. Conrad remained hidden in the encirclement because the flowing, medieval robes made it difficult for anyone behind them to see what had occurred. If no one saw anything until it was too late, the partygoers and their robes did their job. They kept Conrad's companions from intervening.

Conrad ceased reaching out and asking for help, knowing no help would come. His rapidly diminishing lack of oxygen created further concerns, and Conrad struggled to pull the mask off his head to no avail.

Once the partygoers broke their circle up, their comrades filling the dance floor moved to the side, creating a path to Conrad.

Sam, Myra, and Robert noticed the path. They should. The path is meant for them. Upon seeing Conrad struggling on the floor, they ran to him. Anna followed in tow.

The group nearly reached Conrad before partygoers grabbed and held them. Seeing Conrad's plight was fine, but offering any help was unacceptable. It took a bit for that fact to sink in, as the trio (and Anna) appeared more worried about Conrad than pointing fingers at who to blame.

Conrad looked up at his screaming friends. How loudly they screamed, Conrad could only guess. The airtight mask cut off any sounds other than Conrad's panicked breathing. He could barely see anything through the fogging eye slits other than seeing his panicked comrades yelling and struggling to get through the crowd that held them back.

Time stalled until it ran out. Conrad could only half-laugh at Robert's absurd biblical costume and Mayra's Wild West attire. Great movies inspired those outfits.

Conrad ceased finding fleeting humor in his entourage's chintzy costumes when he inhaled and found little air entering his mouth or nostrils. He concentrated his final thoughts on his screaming, panicked colleagues. Conrad also noticed that fellow partygoers barely moved. They found nothing out of the ordinary about his situation. Why would they? The partygoers were a party to it.

The eye slits steamed up entirely, giving the impression of a theater fading to black and a picture coming to an end.

Silent screams came out of Mayra, Robert, and normally stoic Sam's mouths when Conrad fell to the ground and convulsed. The convulsions offered a truly final ending to his maiden silent performance.

Conrad joined the silence when he departed the earth. At least his soul did. The silent body sat unmoving on the floor.

Mayra and Robert screamed in panic while Sam, ever the rock-steady studio boss, maintained his composure. Not that he didn't scream. Sam merely didn't scream in panic. He screamed that he wanted to get out of the mansion. Sam screamed he'd call the police. He screamed everyone would pay.

Sam understood the need to appear in charge when someone else held the upper hand.

The screaming stopped when the trio (Anna never screamed) noticed no partygoers reacted. A collection of costumed mimes blocked the way to the front door, and none of the motion picture team wanted to fight their way through the crowd that sunsetted Conrad.

Sam, Mayra, Robert, and Anna all backed away from the two dozen or so partygoers in front of them. The more than two dozen partygoers behind them cleared a path to something hidden behind a curtain.

Horror. Pure horror ran through the very core of the invited entourage upon witnessing a murder. The horror compounded at the second realization: walking out of the homicidal predicament appeared unlikely. Shock led the talkative guests to bite their collective tongues.

The dance hall's quiet ended when an organ's sounds filled the air. The organ played the music an audience would hear in a movie theater only a few years earlier, mimicking the music accompanying an overblown tragic scene in a silent movie.

The quartet looked down the path the partygoers cleared, and they stared at the curtain.

The curtain started to rise slowly.

The sounds of the organ grew louder as Sam began to howl again about calling the police. The boisterous executive did what he often did - bluff and bully. The crowd of partygoers felt no intimidation. Neither Sam, Robert, Mayra, nor Anna could do anything to overcome the numbers. Sam knew he could only hide his inner terror for so long. No bluff would work.

None of the entourage could overcome the internal panic overwhelming their senses. Outwardly, they didn't fall to pieces because their flight or fight response conned them into believing they could find their way out of the nightmare.

That's what happens to victims caught in these types of scenarios. Or it will happen. Only a few years after the release of the first silent horror film, these scenarios are only starting to play out, at least starting on film.

The four frightened attendees reflexively backed away from the crowd as the partygoers encroached upon them, backing them toward the rising curtain on the other side of the hall.

Sam and his compatriots knew it was futile to keep yelling. Fighting their way through the menacing crowd seemed like a bad and useless idea. Where would they go once they reached the front door? It's not as if it was unlocked.

What about the other door now revealed after the red curtain fully rose?

The organ music increased in volume, drowning all other sounds in the dance hall. None could hear the creaking door open, but they noticed it appeared to open by itself.

The crowd of partygoers pushed the motion picture people to and through the door, which closed once they were on the other side. When the door shut, the organ music stopped.

"Let us out of here, you bastards!" Robert screamed as he banged on the door.

"If they opened it, what would you do?" Sam asked.

Robert attempted to hide how foolish he felt. He shouldn't feel ridiculous about a reaction based on reflexive anger and not-so-hidden fear. Displays of anger hid fear.

"It's a hallway," Mayra noted as she placed her hands on the narrow hall's wall, which led into darkness and an unknown destination.

"Is there anything you'd like to add that we haven't figured out?" Sam had a way of telling people to shut up without directly telling them to shut up.

"The walls have a medieval design." Mayra's comment seemingly ignored Sam's condescension and helped her struggling mind concentrate on something besides the terror she felt.

"We're supposed to care about that because?" Now Robert took a turn at being condescending.

"Because of the way the walls are painted. The grays and the blacks swirl to make them look older," Mayra continued.

"Why would I care about that?" Robert couldn't hide his anger.

"Because you're a set designer," Mayra noted. "I'm surprised you didn't realize these walls are fake."

Robert snapped out of his angry, rude, and internally terrified mode, walked up to the wall, and placed a hand on it. Stone and mortar contributed nothing to the surface. It was all wood. Painted wood. Wood painted to look like an old stone wall.

"He went through a lot of trouble," Sam added.

Anna didn't break her silence by verbally articulating, "Who?" but her facial expression gave her thoughts away.

"Who do you think?" a mind-reading Sam yelled before looking up at the ceiling and screaming, "Creighton! What's this all about? Answer me, Creighton! Drop your gin bottle and come out!"

Organ music began to fill the hallway, which wasn't a real hallway.

"Playing games, Creighton?" Sam bellowed. "What's your game?"

"The fake stone wall looks medieval. Creighton's big on that theme," Mayra pointed out. "***The Menace of the Mansion*** was set in the Middle Ages." The commentary subconsciously furthered an attempt to hide fear as a form of psychological self-preservation.

Robert pushed against the fake wall. It moved slightly, but not much.

Anna wished to feel useful, and all she could think of doing involved mimicking Robert. She walked past him and pressed her hands against the faux wall. It moved. Despite her diminutive weight, Anna's action had an effect. The fake medieval wall had much give. Someone failed to secure the wood flat to the other flats properly.

"Move out of the way." Robert's curt words suggested that if Anna did not move, Robert would step on and over her. Anna wisely moved.

Whether wise or not, Robert gave the weak wooden wall a sharp kick. At least the deliberate action provided the distraction that kept Robert from succumbing to fear.

Unwise, still. The ill-advised swift kick to the standing wall flat brought consequences. The wooden flat, painted to look like an aged wall, broke free from the two sturdier-painted flats on its right and left sides. "Get out of the way!" Sam screamed in Robert's direction. The flat didn't dislodge entirely, but it was hanging in such a way that one more kick would knock it down.

Robert smirked to himself when he saw the reason why the flat came loose so quickly. The set designer knew finishing nails when he saw them and knew far more durable nails were necessary to hold the flat in place.

Anna stood a bit too close to where Robert wanted to kick, so he shoved her out of the way, yelling, "Move!"

Furiously, Robert kicked the hanging flat with a heavy boot, and it collapsed backward. The flat didn't land on the ground as it fell part of the way, landing against the wall - the real wall - that the flat stood in front of.

"Knock that off! They'll all come tumbling down!" Sam's yells and admonishments did not yield any results. Robert pressed and kicked onward.

Shadowy darkness hid what was behind the flat, and an impatient Robert kicked at the half-dislodged fake wall, attempting to break it free - or break it in half. Rage seemed to push Robert, as did impatience and hidden panic. After kicking at the flat some more, he grasped his hands around its edges and tried to pull it free.

The other flats started shimmying and shifting.

"He's not one to listen," Mayra said to Sam, adding, "But you already knew that."

Whatever sturdiness they had previously appeared diminished. Proper nails hold the painted flats in place when they do what they're supposed to: remain still. Set designers and others should know that kicking fake walls will reveal the obvious: they're fake.

Fake walls don't handle well under pressure. The other phony walls started to come tumbling down.

The flats not only caught Robert by surprise when they all dislodged from one another and fell apart and to the ground.

What surprised everyone was how not-so-random the flats collapsed. They collapsed into what seemed like a well-ordered puzzle. A flat here. A flat there.

Several flats fell in front of Sam, Mayra, and Anna. A massive one fell from the ceiling. The mysterious flat of impressive height, length, and width fell in front of the trio's path, blocking their ability to move forward and cutting them off from Robert.

The fallen flats created a barrier between Robert and his colleagues. Randomness no longer seemed random.

The trio couldn't walk to Robert, but they could see him. The fallen, makeshift wall reached up to their shoulders, although Anna had to stand on her tiptoes to see over the thick wooden structure.

All three could see Robert without anything impeding their gaze. How unfortunate, considering what's to come.

"Do I have to kick you three free now?" Robert asked with sarcasm, his back turned to the swaying flats. He should never have turned his back.

A new flat fell from above and hit Robert from behind, knocking him down. The set designer fell face-first, and the falling flat lay on top of him like a stiff blanket. Robert rolled from face down to face up with the heavy flat still on top of him. Robert tried to crawl out from under the weight, which wasn't too heavy. It became heavier when another flat fell on it. The weight increased when someone threw yet another flat on top.

Threw.

The trio's vision didn't extend into the shadows, so they couldn't see who threw the flat. Then, shadowy figures emerged from the darkness between the painted flats and the actual wall into the sparse light from chandeliers overhead.

The partygoers arrived, moving from the dance floor, still dressed in medieval costume wear.

They did not move festively. They moved with purpose. They picked flats up off the ground and began piling them on Robert.

"What are you bastards doing?" Robert couldn't back up with action. The weight and the injury-induced impact from the fallen flat made it impossible for him to move.

"Creighton! Enough!" Sam bellowed, and his screams echoed through the darkness. It's gone too far, you mad bastard!" Sam should have expected the silent treatment from Creighton. Llewellyn Creighton no longer worked for Sam. The studio head could yell as much as he wanted, but he shouldn't expect an immediate or apologetic response.

The odd partygoers filtered out of the darkness and entered the medieval hallway. The tight interior truly seemed like a medieval dungeon's hallway despite being what it was: a makeshift, decorated set perfect for a movie.

"Get these flats off of me!" Robert yelled.

"Move them off of you!" Sam responded to the yell with little sympathy but much urgency.

"My back! The flat hit my back! I can barely move!" Robert's plight seemed terrible and would soon worsen.

The emerging partygoers did not come empty-handed. Nor did they come bearing gifts. Robert assuredly would not refer to the large stones and cinder blocks they held as gifts, even though the partygoers bestowed them on Robert.

They bestowed them on top of Robert.

"What are you God damn lunatics doing?" Robert asked, even though he could see what they were doing. What they started doing wasn't nice. Yes, they nicely started placing the rocks on the flats, but the action proved cruel. Stones and cinder blocks pose heavy weight.

"My Lord," Mayra gasped, realizing the partygoer's plans.

The partygoers in medieval costumes offered more than the celebration of the theme; the theme wasn't a celebration of life, which had little value during medieval times, a theme repeated in the 1920s on silent movie sets.

They spread the rocks and cinder blocks across the 3x7 ft flats unevenly. Situating the natural stone and broken cement at the center of the top flat made the most sense. Underneath the three layers of flats was the one layer of Robert, and the added weight pressed down on the center of his chest.

Robert gasped as the weight increased. Organ music pumping into the scene drowned his gasps as the pressing increased.

Everyone had their pressing issues at the party. Sam wished to press Creighton on returning to his loyal duty as a cash cow. Robert, Conrad, and Mayra wanted to press on and remain in Sam's good graces by accepting their invites. Anna felt shocked at receiving an invite, feeling out of place among her companions - she had no cinema status. Never did. The party invite gave her life value.

Robert figured Sam would find a way to save money by getting free press on a film by luring old Creighton out of retirement. Sam's situation proved pressing since his studio sought a cash influx. What irony that Robert would now die by pressing under a makeshift press.

The silent partygoers had a more retrograde concept of the press and medieval pressing. They stuck with the party's theme and chose to press Robert - not for an answer or a favor, but literally. Robert gasped for air as more rocks and stones joined other rocks and stones on the top flat. The weight increased, and Robert discovered the medieval-themed party strove for incredible authenticity.

The pain, suffering, and torture he endured evoked the lost pastime of execution by pressing. The more weight the partygoers added to the flat, the greater the crushing pressure. Robert found breathing harder and harder.

Like a grand silent epic, the chosen demise for Robert would take a long time to end.

Robert gurgled as blood started coming out of his mouth and ears. Death by pressing gave internal organs their challenges.

Execution by pressing reflected an epic way to die—epic in the cinematic and medieval torture sense. If making a picture, filming the scene from beginning to end required commitment from a production crew, and completing an epic could require weeks of commitment. The same applies to those long-gone characters who performed the execution for real. Death could take weeks.

Tonight's show lacked that kind of budget.

An unnamed contributor devised a running time-reducing end to the scene: a massive cinder block fell from the dark ceiling above and landed on Robert's head.

Who started the trend of using Latin words at the end of a silent movie? Does that trend still exist? If so, the creatives behind Robert's demise could craft title cards reading, "Exactus. Perfectus. Effectus."

Highly educated Robert fleeting thoughts imagined a set prominently displaying a Latin word for his first and final performance, "Vale!" would make little sense to commoners in the audience. The English translation seems better.

Goodbye.

"Creighton! Creighton! Have you lost your mind?" Sam's voice bellowed against the wooden walls of the darkened faux medieval corridor. Sam's voice had no accompaniment as the organ music ceased.

"Browbeating him isn't going to work," Mayra offered unsolicited advice as Anna cowered behind her.

"Creighton!" Sam screamed, ignoring one of the two remaining underlings. "Why are you doing this?"

"You think he'll have to give you a good reason?" Mayra couldn't hide her dismissive attitude toward her, a tone designed to hide her panic. Her tone irked Sam enough to grab her by her costume's collar and pull her close to his face. "You want to die? I don't." Sam's anger and bullying sought to hide the panic he felt but couldn't put up as good of an act as Mayra. She boasted of a career as a former stage actor, not Sam.

Sam let go of Mayra's collar, realizing that agitating an ally wouldn't do him any good in an increasingly hopeless situation.

Sam turned away from Mayra and glanced where the flats blocked his path back to the dance hall. More flats turned upwards and pressed against the ones that fell sideways, blocking the ability to see the door they entered. Sam appreciated the small favor that he could no longer see what remained of Robert on the floor.

The added flats cut off whatever light emitted in front of them. The now dim chandelier light made it possible to see where Sam, Mayra, and Anna stood.

"Creighton," Sam spoke the name in a calmer tone with an attempt at persuasion. "Tell us what this is all about."

"We know what it's about," Mayra added.

Sam didn't acknowledge Mayra's comment and continued to address the host whose presence he felt. "We can work things out, Creighton. It doesn't have to go any further."

"You can't bring his wife back," Mayra noted.

Sam bit his lip, not wanting to lash out at Mayra. What point would that serve? Sam knew Llewellyn Creighton produced and directed all the evening's events. Why bother arguing with a script girl?

"Creighton, please listen," Sam pleaded, unable to hide the fear cracking in his voice.

"Tonight...the...events....we can brush it away."

The dimming lights began to fade further. Sam paid no heed to the diminishing illumination and continued making promises to Creighton. Whether Creighton heard them or not, Sam didn't know.

"You know I'm not lying, Creighton. We can hide what happened tonight." Sam lacked a reputation for truthfulness, but his words came with no lies. He told another truth when he said, "We've hidden a lot of things stars and others did."

"*Fantastique.* Remind him of the stunts and strings you pulled to hush things." Mayra tended to interject when Sam slid off the rails with his promises.

"Do you think he's forgotten about her?" Sam snapped. "Why the hell do you think we're here? Why the hell do you think what happened went and happened?

Mayra took her turn at biting a lip.

"Creighton! It wasn't our fault!" The lights dimmed even further as Sam asserted in the growing darkness. Feint light continued to grow dim.

"***The Menace of the Mansion*** suffered an unavoidable disaster!"

What little light glimmered in the hallway further faded.

"You can't blame us!"

The light faded away when Sam finished his imploring words, and the three stood in utter darkness.

Mayra broke the shrouded silence with terse words. "He blames us."

Sam said nothing and turned his attention toward a mild light glimmering at the end of the hallway.

"I guess he wants us to move along," Mayra deduced correctly.

"I don't give a damn." Sam felt no inclination to humor a madman. Sam stood still, lost in thought. The man knew how to run a decent-sized motion picture studio, but he had no strategy for escaping his current mess.

Sam stared down the long hallway and saw the glimmering light over a door. The door and the light stood apart from the style and look of the hallway, if you could sincerely call it a hallway.

Sam couldn't help but think of such things because he had to scour scripts and film dailies for ridiculous flubs that would ruin a movie. Sam snapped out of his brief daydreaming when he remembered he wasn't standing on a movie set.

His current troubles are real. Sam silently stewed on that reality, ignoring that the dark hallway he found himself was - for all intents - a....

"Movie set," Mayra said. The two words snapped Sam out of his daydream.

"What?" Sam heard Mayra but didn't understand her meaning.

"He built a movie set. Here. In his mansion." Mayra had more to add. "He's mimicking the accident on *The Menace of the Mansion.*"

"You don't think I don't know that already?" Sam held in his fear, as did Mayra, but both quaked inside. Anna said nothing, as always, and she had no ability to hide her fears. The darkness shrouded her anxieties, but Sam and Mayra heard her knees quaking. Not that they cared.

"Sam, you think we should go to the light and through the door?" Mayra had a way of nudging Sam, playing to his ego. Present conditions suggested she speak curtly, but Mayra knew to play to Sam's ego. Sam subconsciously appreciated the approach.

"You want to follow the light and go through the door?" Sam asked the question contemptuously. "Did you notice he killed Conrad and Robert? Don't you think he wants to kill us, too? With your expertise in script continuity, I'd think you'd have the brains to know what's coming - he wants us past that door so he can kill us!" Sam raised his voice enough that it echoed past the remaining fake wall flats and against the real stone walls that comprised much of the mansion.

On cue, sand fell from the ceiling and landed on Sam's shoulder. He brushed the sand off, not that he worried about any harm coming to the Henry VIII costume.

More sand fell, with some landing on Sam's head.

"Are we playing jokes now, Creighton?" Sam yelled in the darkness, unsure what purpose browbeating Llewellyn Creighton would serve.

Mayra rubbed some fallen sand out of her eyes. No sand got in her ears, so she could hear the pebbles and small stones hitting the ground. The sound echoed in the darkness.

"We should move toward the door," Mayra suggested, although her tone sounded more like an order. Sam didn't like to take orders.

"NO!" Sam bellowed, acting as if he were sitting behind his oak desk in his office off Gower Street.

The sound of a large rock falling from the ceiling and hitting the floor next to him reminded Sam that he was not on Gower Street anymore.

More rocks - large rocks - fell from the ceiling.

"Sam, the place's rigged." Mayra pointed out the obvious, not that Sam would accept the obvious. Ego gets in his way.

"No. I'm not playing along with him." A huge rock fell from the ceiling and grazed Sam's arm. The rock missed his foot by an inch. Missing by an inch meant Sam dodged a broken ankle.

"Time to move," Mayra said as her footsteps echoed in the dark, heading toward the door and light. "Unless you want to end up like Creighton's wife and have this whole place fall on top of you."

Play the game or die like my wife. Such thoughts ran through Sam's head as he moved in the direction of the light at the hallway's end.

"Anna!" Sam yelled.

Anna gave a now-hustling Sam a look that acknowledged his acknowledgment of her. Sam noticed he had her attention, so he offered helpful advice.

"Don't get lost."

The other side of the door revealed nothing to encourage the (now) trio to think their situation improved. The door opened to reveal a wooden floor haphazardly built with lumber. Some lumber looked like new pine, while other wood planks reflected aged oak. Two other colors signified different kinds of wood, but the three couldn't decipher them in the dark. Llewelyn Creighton seemed not to care about owning a well-lit mansion, at least not on this night.

"Another door," an exasperated Sam muttered under his breath, adding, "Damn you, Creighton," when he saw another door on the other side of the oddly fitted floor. Sam noticed drawn curtains on the right and left sides of the door frame. Sam finally got the meaning of the love for the doors. The curtains gave it away.

They represented entrances and exits to theaters. The hallways were aisleways like the ones inside a movie theater.

"He expects us to hurry, I believe," Mayra said, intending to nudge Sam. The studio boss didn't intend to swiftly move across the floor to the eventual doom he feared awaited on the other side.

Sam feared the cause of his possible doom: he'd fail to talk Creighton out of whatever nefarious plans the silent movie star turned madman had planned. Sam had a knack for talking Creighton into things, but those conversations focused on getting the actor to accept a role or reduce his salary on a project.

Fear didn't entirely overwhelm Sam because the executive felt he had enough gab skills to sway Creighton away from his lunatic plans. Sam prayed his talents wouldn't fail him, so he put more effort into praying that he'd actually see Creighton face-to-face and not face a cruel death while the actor watched from the shadows.

The oddly slapped-together flooring worried Mayra. Her continuity talents led her to pick up on how the wood plank floor did not connect directly to the walls on the side - a gap existed between the floor and the red curtain-covered walls. Roughly two feet of space existed between the wooden floor's edge and the curtains. The two-foot gap, unsurprisingly, remained shrouded in darkness.

The gap between the narrow floor and the curtains made Sam feel trepidation about walking on the weird wooden surface. Sam could read people and situations. How else would he reach studio boss status in a con artist's profession? Sam knew the hand Creighton dealt had a joker in it. Sam worried about continuing to play the hand, so he kept still, thinking.

Mayra preferred action and took three steps onto the solid wooden floor. She sank slightly but stood solid when she stepped onto another plank. "Rotting. Some planks are rotting. Be careful."

Sam felt his confidence grow after seeing the planks held Mayra's weight - not that he didn't think Creighton had something fatal in mind for them. Poor Sam worried about risking his life playing along with Creighton's game, risking his life by not playing Creighton's game, and looking weak by not taking action and following Mayra's lead. He already felt internal agitation that he was letting a lowly script girl lead him. Lead him, she did. Sam wasn't leading, and somebody had to take action.

"Sam?" Mayra used the executive's name and the suggested question mark to snap him out of his confused internal dialogue.

The studio executive said nothing, but he turned his head off-puttingly as if to seize control and hide fear-frozen legs.

Mayra took charge. "We need to walk. Now."

Sam took several steps forward, not wanting to look scared. He turned to Anna and nastily wondered, "Aren't you coming along?"

Silent Anna followed Sam, who followed Mayra, although he'd never admit he followed anyone. The trio walked about a third of the way without any woes, but woes soon came. The wooden plank floor began to sink under their weight. Sam fell more than a few feet behind his comrades. He'd say prudence told him to fall back.

The floor did more than creak as the three walked about seven feet down the 20-foot hall. The floor began to sway left to right and right to left. The floor moved because it wasn't a floor.

"A bridge," Mayra realized.

"A damn bridge? Over what?" Sam needed to know.

The wooden plank bridge swayed violently when Sam took too hard a step back. Anna stood near the left edge, and with no barrier to keep her from falling off the side, she would have fallen into the darkness below had Mayra not grabbed her by the collar.

"Keep still." Mayra's suggestion was not anything Sam would argue against. The executive stopped moving.

"How far down do you think the fall is under the bridge?" Sam wondered.

"Far enough to do the job Creighton wants to do." Mayra only guessed with her response, but it was a good guess. "I think we should keep moving forward. Slowly." That's more good advice, it seems.

Anna and Sam followed not only Mayra's lead but also her cadence. Mayra moved carefully and deliberately, hoping to reach the end of the 20 feet without running into any surprises. She never entertained the all-too-optimistic idea that Creighton had no surprises planned.

Sam's scream caught her attention and gave her a surprise.

"God damn him!" Sam yelled as his right foot went right through a rotted board. The boards connected to the rotted one were solid, and the single section of rot proved wide enough to swallow Sam's leg. A reflex action told Sam to bend at the knees. Good. His oversized rear landed on a mercifully solid section of wood behind him. Anger snapped Sam out of his shock, and he began to pull his leg from the hole.

The bridge swayed as Sam pulled his leg out.

"Slow down!" Mayra admonished.

Sam couldn't stand Mayra taking the lead from him, and the studio head bristled because she knew better than him how to navigate the situation. As a "script girl," Mayra's duties on a movie set involved keeping a careful eye on continuity. She had to know where everything was between shots to ensure an actor wasn't six inches to the left from a potted plant in the background on a closeup and three inches during a medium shot.

Sam's visits to movie sets involved little more than making a show of himself to the stars and crew while letting his presence known to any lady actors and staff low on the movie studio pecking order. That Sam.

Sam still hated following Mayra's lead, even though the only people seeing him do so were Mayra and the unassuming Anna. Still, as a studio executive, Sam knew the dangers of not looking like being in charge.

Sam knew now wasn't the time for ego and arrogance because he didn't know how far the drop from the bridge was.

Sam pulled his leg out of the hole and crawled forward a foot on what he hoped would be stable boards. Sam despised the mere seconds he spent crawling, so he rushed to rise to a standing position.

"Slow!" Mayra again admonished when Sam's abrupt movement caused the bridge to sway. Sam gave her a death stare.

"Move along," Sam responded in a way that sounded like an order.

Mayra gave her boss a sneaky death stare and uttered no words. She looked at Anna and gave a "come along" motion with her head.

Come along, Anna did. Sam did the same but with less compliant body language.

The trio reached the halfway point to the second door before hearing a creaking sound and feeling a pronounced sinking motion.

The bridge creaked loudly - very loudly - and it sank heavily under the trio's weight.

The odd bridge sank a good six inches, enough for Sam and Mayra to stop moving. Being so diminutive, Anna didn't think shifting her weight slightly forward would cause much harm.

Anna got it wrong.

The bridge sank further, and the sounds of cracking wood echoed.

"Back up! Back up!" Mayra yelled, remembering their footing kept solid two or three steps behind them.

Sam jumped backward, mercifully landing on a solid piece of lumber. His weight caused the bridge to sway. Mayra almost lost her footing. She could barely hold in contempt for her impetuous boss when she mock-condescendingly shouted, "Slowly!"

No one moved. Even the swaying bridge came to a stop after what seemed like a hundred years.

"Move again. Slowly," Mayra repeated.

"How about we backtrack off this damn bridge fast before it falls apart?" Sam bellowed.

"And step on something rotted or broken?" Mayra's responding question brought up a good point.

"I'll lead," Mayra exclaimed. Lead she did. Sam and Anna followed her. What seemed like forever passed before the trio traced their steps back to the starting point.

Sam put his hand on the knob of the door and turned it.

"Locked," Sam stated the obvious.

Organ music began to fill the strange hall.

"He's playing house music." Mayra took her turn to state what had become obvious. "It's a show to him, a picture show. He's playing theater house music for a picture show."

Scant light broke the darkness ahead. The door at the bridge's other end opened, seemingly by itself.

"I didn't write this script, but I think I know the story." Mayra felt a little proud about coming up with a line like that under the present circumstances.

"Cross the bridge or stay here and rot." Sam volleyed back. "Or crack up the damn bridge and fall into God knows what."

Sam and Mayra stared at each other, wondering about their next move. Both caught movement out of the corner of their eyes.

Anna raised her hand, holding up three fingers while shaking her head. "No." Then, she folded two fingers, leaving a single digit raised.

Anna didn't need to speak aloud to snap Sam and Mayra back to attention, proving even a bit player could contribute something to a show.

Mayra articulated Anna's suggestion. "We went together. Maybe we should go one at a time."

"Go," Sam ordered Anna. After all, she's the smallest and lightest. If the bridge cannot hold her weight, it assuredly would not hold the weight of all three.

Young Anna did as told - five words served as a bio to her brief career. Fear ran up her chilled spine. No guarantees existed that the last foot or two of the bridge had no surprises. Neither Conrad nor Robert found a way out of their predicaments. Old Creighton made sure of that. Or did he?

If there was a way out, Conrad and Robert were too dumb to see it.

That thought ran through Mayra's head, and she tried to see hope in the nightmare she had found herself in. Worse for her, she found herself in a nightmare scenario with utter incompetents. That type of scenario remained a recurring nightmare during her career.

She had little respect for Conrad, Robert, Sam, and a cavalcade of obnoxious men who comprised the motion picture industry of the early 1930s. Mayra felt further agitated at the lack of respect for her script continuity talents. "Script girl" was such a boorish credit to receive, one that didn't tell the tale of her duties.

Mayra snapped back to the present when she realized Anna moved too slowly and appeared too worried about stepping on something that would break.

Mayra's mind returned to the here and now, but her constant underlying anger powered her actions. She yanked Anna by the collar and pulled her backward. "Come back," Mayra quipped with annoyance, "I'll do it."

With deliberate poise and grace, Mayra walked across the bridge. She slowed a little in spots, deliberately thinking about her next move. Some boards looked rotted, and she wouldn't make the mistake of stepping on them.

The open door was a mere five feet away, and Mayra would soon reach it.

Things went too easy. If only Mayra had acknowledged the "too easy" part before hands reached out from underneath the bridge on both sides. The hands and accompanying arms extended from the flowing medieval robes, revealing the partygoers.

The returning partygoers had an odd task. They pulled some lumber boards from their place on the bridge. They grabbed pine, oak, and other wooden lumber planks and began moving them around, doing so in front of and behind Mayra.

Crossing a bridge became a game, and the rules and landscape changed.

The bridge's plank configuration also changed, creating a dire conundrum for the continuity girl. She remembered where it was safe to step, but did she remember the color of the safe wooden planks or any odd markings on them? Of all professionals, wouldn't a script continuity girl notice such things? Or did she let her mind wander when she should've been paying attention?

Mayra should have expected the arms coming from under the bridge to mess up her job. Those same arms previously held the bridge in place to prevent swaying and maintain the element of a surprising shock.

The job fell on Mayra's shoulders and hers alone. Creighton chose to test her, and she had no option but to take the test. Waiting to starve in the dark seemed like the only option, with one door locked and the only open one twenty feet away across a prop ridge — and prop it was.

Prop or not, an open door meant a way forward. Who knew how long it would remain open?

Mayra recognized the design as partially constructed for function and primarily for show. The bridge represented the type you'd find on a movie set. The construction looked fine, but the bridge utterly lacked sturdiness.

Did you need sturdiness when the bridge existed only for film purposes?

Yes. That single affirmative word ran through Mayra's head. Yes, because real people - actors and crew - would have to walk on it.

Perceptive, Mayra finally saw the underlying theme of Creighton's plot.

The flaws reminded her of how they built the sets on *The Menace of the Mansion*. Build everything fast. Build everything inexpensively. Make sure it looks good. Forget about function. We'll tear it down after the shoot.

All bad ideas, as Llewelyn Creighton and his late wife would attest.

Mayra expected a curveball, but she knew enough to play the game. Creighton never struck her as someone with an inflated opinion of greatness. Mayra believed she'd one-up the faded box office star by finding her way out of the mess.

Not that she would expect Creighton to give her any credit.

When she heard a noise behind her, Mayra had an unfortunate feeling that she underestimated Llewelyn Creighton.

Mayra looked over her shoulder and saw the hands from underneath the bridge. They reached for boards that comprised the bridge. Anyone involved with motion picture continuity picks up on things. Mayra should have noticed no one nailed down the boards.

So it proved easy for the previously absent partygoers to pull away random boards, leaving a massive gap behind Mayra, one she wouldn't dare try to jump over.

Forward or bust.

Organ music continued to fill the air, growing louder. Mayra looked back at Sam and Anna, but they couldn't do anything for her.

Mayra figured things worsened when she heard the door creaking. She turned her head back toward the door ahead she was supposed to reach to see it begin to close. Mayra wisely concluded that she needed to get to the door before it shut, or Creighton's picture show would have a flat, abrupt twist ending.

Creighton had more to offer silent cinema than his pantomime acting skills. It seems he could script a silent movie and get the story across without anyone saying a word.

Mayra glanced down at the floorboards in front of her, roughly five or six feet worth, still less than the gap behind her. Any foolish ideas about leaping over the chasm to her rear flank swiftly drifted out of her head.

Mayra spent a split second too much time looking over her shoulder at the chasm between her current position and the missing bridge section behind her. She should have kept her eyes ahead of her. By the time she snapped out of her daydreams and turned to the front, the lights had gone out.

She could still move forward to the door. Nothing obstructed her path. However, she had to choose her path wisely since she only had her memory to guide her to the closing door. Where were the gaps, and what boards suffered from severe rot?

Was the script girl paying attention?

Darkness soon enveloped Mayra as she stood on her perch - if you wish to call it a perch. A partial bridge held up mysteriously is a better description. Mayra knew there was nothing mysterious about why the bridge didn't collapse or fall apart. The costumed partygoers likely held it in place somehow. Or, a person skilled with the late Robert's exquisite set design talents may have devised a unique special effect with the bridge. He was so good with that in most of his films. ***The Menace of the Mansion*** represented an anachronistic departure from his usual high-quality work.

Now, it made sense.

Mayra deduced what Creighton had devised. She might not know the how, but she knows the why.

If her life didn't hang in the balance of Creighton's demented mind, Mayra would smirk at her ability to deduce everything. She'd take much self-satisfaction from knowing she determined the score long before the all-knowing mighty studio executive named Sam.

Sam needed to be fed information more than he'd care to admit. Don't expect anyone to call the pompous ass on his shortcomings, either.

Mayra had to be delicate about informing Sam about what time it was. Lord, that man took up so much space in her head that she forgot about her worsening predicament.

Mayra heard the sound of a wood plank behind her come loose and fall. For a second, she thought it floated in the air somehow. The plank made no landing sound. Then, it made a landing sound. The delayed reaction suggested one long, far fall. If a plank could fall behind her, the ones ahead could fall. The same goes for the ones under her. She needed to act quickly and get across the remainder of the bridge before her.

What a simple plot to follow! All Mayra needed to do was step on the boards able to hold her weight. She just had to remember where they were.

Creighton. You're as rotten as Sam in your own way.

Where were those planks that looked so impressively solid?

"Mayra! Mayra! Where are you?" Sam bellowed in the darkness. Worry bled through all his words.

"I'm not going to leave you, Sam," Mayra replied, knowing Sam worried more about being alone in future chapters of this adventure if anything happened to her.

"I can't see you anymore!" Sam further exasperated his worries, standing in his spot in the dark.

"Pitch darkness does that," Mayra replied with rare overt sarcasm toward her boss. "And stop breaking my concentration."

"ARE YOU PLAYING A GAME HERE!" Sam screamed out of frustration.

"Yes," Mayra responded, "I'm playing Creighton's game. Don't you get it?"

Mayra heard nothing else besides light organ music. Sam failed to reply to her response because he didn't know what to say.

"Conrad made costumes. Robert built sets." Mayra paused before adding, "I was in charge of continuity. Get it?"

"NO!" Sam had that obnoxious and clueless way about him.

"Script girls. Continuity. That's the predicament," Mayra droned with a serious undertone. "I have to remember the good planks, like a good script girl."

Conrad needed to make costumes that fit but did not restrict mobility. Robert had to build sturdy sets.

Mayra snapped out of her internal monologue when she heard another piece of lumber falling behind her. Closer than the last one, suggesting she better move.

Move, she did. Mayra knew waiting wouldn't make her any better at her task. She should have an eye and a memory for continuity between shots. The top script girl should have that same eye now, knowing where to step. Hopefully, she didn't let her mind drift when looking ahead of the bridge like she did during the production of *The Menace of the Mansion*. True, she focused more on the epic production next on her agenda after that miserable horror picture.

Not an acceptable excuse for a star of Creighton's magnitude.

Mayra took a step forward.

Creighton, how did we sell your talents short?

Sam didn't think of those words. They traveled through Mayra's thoughts. Despite her limited time to cross the remaining bridge in the dark, she couldn't get Creighton out of her head. She marveled at his skills. What else was there for her to do? Panic wouldn't make the situation better. Mayra lucked out with her first step, landing on a solid plank. Finding another solid plank depended on stepping on a plank based on the image - the map - forming in her head.

You're so much more than silly costumes and gruesome makeup, Creighton.

Of all the thoughts Mayra could entertain in her head, she chose to think of the mad brilliance of a reclusive (and homicidal) movie star.

Another step in the darkness. Another good step. Mayra stepped on another solid plank. Proper footing complemented thoughts that should drift back to earlier points in her life. Is that not what people facing death do?

Those facing certain death might think such things. Mayra didn't see death as certain. Yes, she knew she was in a dangerous spot. One wrong step likely meant a long, long fall. And certain death.

Mayra felt certain death had to wait a little longer. As brilliant as he was, Creighton, like many Hollywood stars, remained anchored to his ego. Mayra would only fail Creighton's death trap game if she failed to remember the safe spots and where she needed to step.

Oh, Creighton, you sell me so short.

Mayra knew Hollywood egos. What a shame no Hollywood types gave her a task beyond "script girl" work. She'd make a great producer. She felt stuck in her continuity role, but Mayra knew she was damn good at it.

"Mayra!" Sam yelled from the other side of the darkness. "Are you alright? What's going on."

"Until you hear my body crash to the floor, assume I'm fine!" Mayra didn't appreciate Sam breaking her concentration. "So stop breaking my concentration!"

Sam bit his lip. Mayra refocused on the image of the bridge before the lights went out. If only that miserable organ music would stop playing.

Mayra took a deep breath, knowing she only had so much time to complete her task. The sound of a wood plank hitting the floor made her realize Creighton added a trick to keep her moving.

Damn you, Creighton. Play fair.

The sound of the door closing in front of her furthered the notion she had to keep moving. Pondering her next step had no upsides.

Creighton. Do you think I'll forget where to step?

Mayra didn't rush into moving forward. She knew she needed to be deliberate. Rushing never helped her cause on a movie set. Accuracy did. Many other traits enabled her to perform her job the right way. What a shame she never received all the credit she deserved for her many talents.

There lay the reason why hating Creighton was outside her feelings. Creighton had so many subtle skills outside mugging for the camera as a movie monster. Mayra's talents as a continuity person - a script girl - ensured she paid strict attention to everything.

Not that Mayra didn't feel sharp anger toward Creighton. He blamed her for his wife's death just as he blamed the others who failed to do their jobs properly. Mayra felt indignant that Creighton assumed she cut corners when relaying info to talent and crew because she looked ahead to a prestige epic, not Creighton's bloated star vehicle.

She'd show old Creighton. Mayra would shove the damn game he laid up down his throat one step at a time.

Time kept running out, so Mayra took another step.

Solid ground, her foot landed not.

Sam heard the boards fall apart. He heard Mayra scream in shock.

She fell through the bridge to her end. That's all. Who'd expect more? Creighton never liked supporting performers to upstage him.

Sam spent less time on movie sets than he initially believed. As a studio mogul, he did what so many executives did. Sam spent hours and hours in his office at the studio and hours upon hours entertaining business partners (and would-be business partners) at social affairs. Don't forget the watering holes. Hollywood had no shortage of functional alcoholics, and Sam found himself hopping from nightclub to nightclub (and disreputable bar to disreputable bar) to close deals with actors, directors, writers, and others.

What Sam did not do was spend as much time on movie sets. Sure, he popped in occasionally, usually with a photographer in tow. However, the notion that Sam was an active producer in films that bore his name in giant, bold letters was fiction. Sam loved fiction since newspapers presented it as nonfiction, but fiction it was.

Had Sam spent more time on a film set, he wouldn't have felt as down as he did when Mayra's body hit the floor an unknown number of feet below the bridge. The grizzled executive grew familiar with seeing finished films at screenings. He never saw how they edited in the sound effects - an odd scenario, considering how revolutionary sound in films became.

Sam wasn't about the revolution. He was about putting the key players together and selling the film. He did that so well!

Sam liked bombast, and movie shoots lacked all the hoopla a finished film delivered.

Mayra's demise lacked bombast. Had her fall from grace (and the bridge) been captured on film, they could have done something to spice it up in the editing room.

When it hit the mysterious floor below, the sound she made - or her body made better fit a silent movie. In a sound feature, audiences would expect bombastic sound. Even audiences who frequented the low-budget, poverty-row B-movies expected decent sound effects. A middling "thud" wouldn't cut it, even if the cinematographer perfectly captured the shock on Mayra's face when she stepped on a plank that couldn't support her weight.

A skilled and cruel cinematographer could capture a close-up of Mayra's face when she realized her life would soon expire. Mayra had an acting background, although she rarely spoke about it. Imagine an inspired actor's overly dramatic facial expression attempting to convey the misery of knowing one's life ends now. Oh, the regrets. Who wouldn't have regrets at the moment of their passing?

The damn "thud" Mayra's body made when it hit the ground would have drawn laughter from audiences expecting more. They paid a dime for a ticket. They deserve something more than a miserable "thud."

As Sam witnessed those thoughts flashing through his head, the executive gained a newfound appreciation for silent films. Sam lacked a solitary fiber in his body that anyone would call sentimental. The studios made silent movies because nobody knew how to record sound. When savvy characters in the industry learned how to record sound, they recorded it. Things changed. Actors who found themselves out of work had to deal with their predicament.

Audiences wouldn't hear how Mayra's body sounded when it landed on the floor. Would it matter that her death would end silently? Would not the look on her expiring face tell the tale best?

None of that mattered now. It never did. Tonight's events played out in real life, not on film, silent or otherwise. Mayra's gone, and Sam's on his own.

Or was he? No, Sam had Anna to keep him company on his journey. Sam knew the journey would be fatal unless Creighton's talents ran dry.

When the chandelier light returned, Sam didn't know what to make of the rope bridge connected to cables hanging from the ceiling. He had no idea how Creighton set all this up—a split second passed before Sam figured out how Creighton did it. He didn't do it. A star (or former star) of Creighton's magnitude knows many people. Apparently, he knew enough disturbed Hollywood set workers that he found someone who could craft a makeshift rope bridge for Sam to cross over the chasm that took Mayra's life.

Where would he find such a disgruntled and demented crew?

Didn't matter. Other pressing issues ran through Sam's mind. The executive had to cross the rope bridge to reach the door and face the music. Sam chuckled to himself in a defeated way as he listened to Creighton's returning organ music. Sam never liked organ accompaniments and despised listening to them in theaters only a few years earlier during the (exclusively) silent era.

Sam looked at Anna, and she took the hint and led the way. Her lighter weight handled the rope bridge reasonably well, and Sam would be lying if he said his heart didn't sink when his body sank worse upon stepping on the rope bridge.

Anyone who'd accuse Sam of cowardice by "suggesting" Anna lead the way before him didn't see things Sam's way.

Sam knew he was the big star of Creighton's show.

Seriously. Would Creighton save Anna for last?

She's going before him in the tragic and the who-crosses-the-bridge-first sense.

Creighton would finish her off first. Sam didn't wish any bad things would happen to Anna, but he'd be lying if he said he didn't appreciate the extra time to deduce a way out of his predicament.

Deducing proved complicated.

"Keep going!" Sam rudely shouted at Anna when she looked at him, wondering if she should continue forward. Sam shook his head, not understanding why Anna had trepidation about walking through the door once they reached the end of the rope bridge.

What are we going to do, girl? Stand here forever?

Those thoughts ran through Sam's head as he wondered what lay beyond.

Crossing the door's threshold gave him no answers, as the dark passageway led to a dark stairwell - a circular, twirling, descending stairwell that led deep to the nether regions of the mansion.

Sam could see little ahead of him as he walked down the spiral staircase to the lower levels. The "little" included a light off in the distance, shining where the stairwell ended.

Sam kept behind Anna the bulk of the way. After all, if the script called for her to die before his "performance," what did Sam have to lose by confronting his host at this early juncture?

Sam felt no shock when looked beyond the stairwell's end. He saw what he expected to see: someone playing the organ.

The music filled the strange room at the lower level of the mansion's basement. The organ player never turned or looked over his shoulder to glance at Anna and Sam as they continued down the stairs.

Sam had no trouble recognizing the organ player, even though the organist turned his back to Sam and Anna.

The player was Llewellyn Creighton, all decked out in his Black Death costume from *The Menace of the Mansion*.

Anyone who thought the spiral staircase leading to Llewellyn Creighton's mansion's basement would be adorned in cobwebs never met the host. Creighton had his quirks, as did all movie stars of his stature, and he had an unnatural love for neatness and order.

The stairwell had no cobwebs or dust. Someone took daily care of it, a fact that traveled through Sam's head as he descended the stairwell slowly. Sam felt perturbed about Anna's fast walking. She seemed almost in a rush to reach the bottom and meet the real-life Menace of the Mansion. Not that they didn't meet previously. Anna had a minor part in that disastrous production but significant enough to catch Creighton's attention.

Sam had no desire to reach the end of the steps, but steps - and lives - end at some point. Sam worried that his life would soon expire, thanks to Creighton's madness.

The organ music grew louder the further Sam descended the stairwell. Why wouldn't it? The further Sam traveled, the closer he came to the organ and the organ player.

When Sam finally arrived at the final step, he could see the grandiose organ and the organist.

Llewellyn Creighton.

Sam's eyes narrowed on the rude host, who kept his back turned to him. Creighton seemed more interested in playing the organ while wearing the ominous Black Death costume the Menace of the Mansion wore in the fatal movie of the same name.

Time stopped. Sam waited. Creighton never turned to face his guests. Guests. Don't forget Anna.

If Creighton had a proper audience, they would appreciate the organ music. The actor had talent. He practiced playing the organ in the basement during his years of Hollywood exile.

Creighton focused on two things in the aftermath of the disaster on **The Menace of the Mansion**: mastering the organ and planning revenge for his wife's death.

At present, Creighton appeared more interested in playing the organ than taking revenge on Sam or Anna.

"Creighton," Sam intoned, "Why don't you take off that ridiculous outfit and state what you want."

Creighton continued to play the organ with one hand as his other hand responded to Sam's directive. His right hand pulled off the Black Death doctor's mask, although Sam couldn't see the retired actor's face.

Sam kept his distance until anger overtook him. The executive neared Creighton cautiously, not getting too close but close enough to engage his host.

Engage, he did, in the most direct and discourteous of ways.

"Creighton," Sam intoned the name the way a boss spoke to an underling. "What the hell am I supposed to do about your wife? The damn set collapsed."

Creighton never missed a note while playing the organ.

"Creighton, let's say I didn't care about your wife's well-being. Do you think I'd want bad press?"

The host kept playing the organ, offering no verbal response. The current organ piece ended, and Creighton seamlessly moved on to the next one.

"Creighton!" Sam bellowed. "What's this all about?!"

Without taking a breath, Creighton responded. "My wife. Me. And you."

The still-great actor delivered the six short words with perfect inflection and tone. Few would expect such delivery from a silent movie star. Granted, Creighton wasn't acting.

He continued to play the organ, filling the dark basement with grim music.

"You want to blame me for an accident?" Sam asked.

"I blamed more than you alone."

"I noticed."

Creighton did something he rarely did. He laughed. He laughed at Sam's line and any thoughts that Sam cared that three people met their end. Studio executives. Ice water. Veins.

"It was an accident, Creighton. An accident."

Creighton tapped the organ keys, keeping his back turned. Finally, Creighton replied to his guest with an effective delivery,

"Shoddy set building by a know-it-all designer. Poor-fitting costumes that restricted movement during an unforeseen emergency. A script girl so disinterested she never saw problems on the set that suggested dangers. How terrible it was to ignore concerns that elaborate balconies couldn't hold the weight of all the actors crammed into their poorly constructed and cramped spaces."

Creighton never stopped playing the organ as he turned to look over his shoulder at Sam, saying, "Lots of people were at fault for that set collapsing. Every one of them worked for you, Sam."

Since Creighton only partially turned to look at Sam, Sam only partially saw the burn marks and scars that altered Creighton's appearance. It's been a while since Sam looked directly at Creighton. Sam forgot how jarring Creighton's face could appear.

"'Thrifty' Sam, what a proper name everyone around town had for you," Creighton said over his shoulder. "Some things they call you are less catchy and far ruder." The former silent star cracked a terse smile that raised Sam's blood pressure.

Creighton tilted his head back to face the organ fully. The actor never missed a keystroke on the massive instrument. He didn't need to face Sam for the executive to hear what he had to say. Creighton had a skill for emoting.

"'Thrifty' Sam knows how to keep a budget low, even on grand-scale glorious productions! 'Thrifty' Sam knew how to take risks. Oh, the money he saved on those odd and amazing-looking gothic productions! Safety? Oh, 'Thrifty' Sam never cut costs while weighing the risks." Creighton failed to hide his glowing anger at the executive. "The risks always weighed low on Sam's magic scale."

"For a silent movie star, you have a way of running your mouth," Sam lobbied back with an insolent tone.

"Funny. Never knew you could speak so well or knew so many words."

"I can say a lot of things, Sam." A pause. "I only preferred to never say much to you." Creighton knew how to get under Sam's skin.

Sam bristled angrily, but the executive knew how to keep his cool. That's a trick he learned long ago when starting in the theater back when the theater was all you had.

Sam's rough upbringing on the other side of the country taught him to play things cool. The portly executive wanted to pummel and strangle Creighton, but he knew not to rush into anything. Sam didn't know what game Creighton wanted to play. He only knew he was in a bad situation, serving as a pawn in whatever deviousness the silent movie madman had in mind.

"You don't seem nervous, Sam. Always the poker face. I know you're scared, Sam. I guess you don't want to seem weak. That's awful for a studio head, right?" Creighton didn't expect Sam to answer. He was right.

"I don't think I'm next up on your show of shows," Sam spoke with conviction as his eyes diverted to quiet Anna standing off to the side with a catatonic expression.

"Why do you say that?"

"Because you won't save the finale for a 19-year-old mute who played a damn background extra."

"She had one nice moment in the film."

"Fine. *Featured extra.*"

"I'm a professional actor and an amateur musician, Sam. I don't plot stories like the screenwriters," Creighton continued to play the organ, again looking over his shoulders to face Sam. "And you're no detective. Or else you'd have picked up on things earlier."

Anna moved from where she stood. The diminutive girl walked to Creighton and sat beside him at the organ. Creighton stopped playing the instrument with both hands and used only his left. Anna's right hand tapped on the organ keys. Creighton and Anna made a fantastic duo. They played music together so well.

Sam felt his heart nearly explode from anxiety. It looks like he has less time than he thought.

Sam tried to process Creighton's words. He couldn't, so the great actor fed lines.

"She gamed you, Sam. She gamed all of you." Creighton turned to Anna and smiled. She returned a smile to him. Creighton added, "An underappreciated actress."

"She led Conrad to where I wanted him on the dance floor. She tapped on the wall flat that I wanted Robert to kick. She conned Mayra to lead the way on the bridge. She walked ahead of you, making you think she'd be the next sacrifice you'd have to witness." Creighton didn't turn to face Sam with his following comment. He knew it would bite more if he didn't look. "Sam. He's not only thrifty, he's slick. That New York edge helped him with the Bohemians in California. God bless, old Sam. He could look at you and tell you what time it was. Except when he couldn't see the clock."

"Nervous?" Creighton asked his nervous guest. "Foolish question. It's not like you can act nervous."

"Tell me what the hell you want, Creighton." Sam feigned steadfastness. Or did he? Sam had a penchant for giving orders under all circumstances.

"What I want, you either can't or won't give."

"WHAT DO YOU WANT?" Sam's nervous and extreme agitation portrayed no act.

"Contrition, Sam. Contrition," Creighton replied while continuing to play the organ one-handed. He glanced at Anna, who continued to offer the other hand that made beautiful organ music. Creighton smiled at Anna, who was expressionless and silent. The one-time star returned attention to Sam, suggesting, "I don't think I'll ever receive any repentance from you. At least not anything sincere. I'd get the lying and game-playing you're used to delivering to talent, crew, and office help."

Sam took a deep breath, readying himself to take action. Before he could lunge at Creighton, the host said something that gave Sam quite a pause.

"I want you to act."

"Huh?" Sam's East Coast background snuck into his response.

"Act. It's not as easy as it sounds. My wife felt so overwhelmed. No surprise. She didn't like appearing on film, but I did what I could to boost her confidence - oh, foolish me. I believe I share some of the blame. Unlike you and your colleagues, I had sleepless nights when the set - the elaborate set! - collapsed on her.

"Guilt. Oh, the guilt." Creighton's oratory skills were so underrated.

Creighton looked at Anna. "She'll tell you how hard acting is. Poor girl froze in front of the camera, but you saw promise in her, among other things. My wife could have dodged the collapsing set but ran to push frozen little Anna out of the way. Poor, quiet Anna struggled with guilt ever since. That's not something you'd know about."

"Creighton, I'm done with you!" Enough. Sam had enough. He lunged at Creighton, grabbed him by his absurd costume's collar, and spun him around. Sam finally saw Creighton's scarred visage.

Sam saw what he saw - a menace.

Creighton put up no fight when Sam's thick fingers wrapped around his throat. Sam squeezed tightly. Creighton's eyes bugged open as his former boss cut off his air.

Anna turned to watch the unfolding drama. Her eyes opened wide while her face remained stoic. She offered Creighton no assistance.

Whether Anna intended to help or not mattered little. What could she do? It seemed as if nothing could break Sam's grip.

"Want me to act? How about I play music?" Sam mockingly asked as he banged Creighton's head against the organ's keys. The previously ominous and eloquent organ music no longer filled the dark underbelly of the mansion. Grotesque banging against the keys replaced the artful sounds.

One. Twice. Thrice. Sam continued to bang Creighton's head against the keys. Sam only stopped to retighten the grip around Creighton's throat. As much as Sam wished to keep punishing his once top star, the studio head wanted to end the show.

Only an act of God would release Sam's grip. That's how much rage Sam felt. The rage overtook his previously hidden fear. While an act of God appeared absent, a three-foot piece of lumber made its presence known. The lumber hit Sam hard across his back, hard enough to make him let go of Creighton and fall to....

"One knee?" Creighton gasped as the air returned to his lungs. "How contrite."

Sam felt a sharp pain in his back where the lumber struck him. He looked to see who hit him with it, but no assailant stood behind him. While stunned, Sam realized he had to look in another direction. Up.

Sam peered upward to the ceiling for the first time. What he saw, he should have expected. A balcony not unlike the one crafted for *The Menace of the Mansion* set ran around the four walls about thirty feet above.

The balcony housed an audience - the costumed partygoers returned. They behaved like an unruly audience ready to throw tomatoes, except they had pieces of wood, discarded metal, rocks, and other things more dangerous than rotten vegetables in their hands.

Sam would have exploded with anger if he could. Getting hit by another piece of lumber - followed by a small rock - took the edge off his anger, replacing it with returning dread. Sam could barely remember what happened a minute ago but knew why he was on his knees. Something a partygoer threw hit him hard enough in the head to drop him to the ground.

Sam tried to stand, but he had a hard time keeping his balance.

"Onward, Sam! It's your call time!" Creighton said the words with a mocking intonation, perfect for the coming radio revolution or the past era of theater. His voice may be fantastic for sound movies, but Creighton's heart remained faithful to the old days of silent films, old days that were only five or so years ago.

A light shined from above, highlighting the spot where Creighton wanted Sam to humiliate himself. Sam finally got an answer to his demanding questions.

What's this all about Creighton? What's your game, Creighton?
Humiliation.

Humiliation acted as an added payoff to Creighton's show. The one-time star had enough humility to admit that a supporting actor helped carry the show.

Anna. What fine supporting talent she provided!

Sam felt personal humiliation because he had failed to grasp her role. He used to be a good judge of people's true intentions.

Sam also used to be a top studio executive, but his fall to the mansion's basement floor mimicked the humiliation of his fallen career.

Sam now had far greater woes than the ones associated with producing B-movies. He peered upward to see where the light came from. Sam saw the glare from the balcony above. He couldn't make out the light setup, but it was better suited for film sets than theaters. That's why the light didn't look as good as it should in the current environment.

Old Sam liked to tell crew members how to do their jobs. He knew how to tell directors how to direct and actors how to act.

When Sam looked up at the weird, masked partygoers looking down on him, he realized how hard all those jobs were. Pleasing an audience has its challenges. He also determined that "partygoers" and "audience" failed as adequate descriptions of those standing on the balconies when a bottle hit the ground and exploded at his feet. Sam knew he stood in the presence of a violent mob awaiting a public execution.

"Onward, good Sam! The spotlight - and fame - await!"

Sam found Creighton's dialogue stilted, but it would fit perfectly with most films playing in moving picture houses today. While Sam acquiesced to Creighton's melodramatic commands, he refused to crawl into the spotlight.

"Contrition Sam! Contrition! That's all I want you to portray! Believably!" Creighton made his directions known again, and Sam stumbled into the spotlight, unsure what to do.

A wood plank landed near Sam's feet, nudging him to get on with the show. Throwing objects at an actor would be a horrible way to direct, but audiences often felt they knew more than directors. Sam looked at the audience above and saw only statue-like stillness from them. He turned his head and his eyes toward Creighton, and the once great silent star yelled, "Contrition!"

Sam only shook his head "No," not out of defiance, but frustration with the maddening scenario.

"Sam," Creighton rolled the executive's name, which didn't hide its intention: a warning.

If anything drove the point further than Creighton's single-word comment, the overhead spotlight that crashed by Sam's side sent a loud message - on with the show, or the show ends now.

Sam accepted his chances of survival were slim, but ever the dealmaker, he believed he could talk his way out of this nightmare provided he played along. Sam hoped for a happy ending to Creighton's mischief and a way back home to his big house on an even bigger hill.

Sam looked in Anna's direction and only stared at an emotionless gaze. Finally, Sam read her. Little Anna felt wracked with guilt.

Their eyes locked for a second, but something broke the gaze—a piece of brick. The brick grazed Sam's head but hit him with enough force to knock him to the ground again. Sam brought his hand to his forehead to rub away the pain. He felt something sticky on his palm. In the light, there were no surprises. Blood covered Sam's palm.

"Emote without words, good Sam!" Creighton exclaimed with bristling enthusiasm. The once great silent star relished the director's role, which he may pick up in the weeks or months following the finale to Sam's performance—not that it was much of a performance. That's not to hint that Sam lacked skill. Creighton asked little of his performer.

"Contrition, Sam!" Creighton repeated the words that made little sense to Sam, and the executive did nothing. He merely looked at Creighton, mouth agape, worried. Something whizzed past Sam's head and bounced off the ground with a clank. Sam glanced at the ground to see a metal cup bounce three times before disappearing from where the above spotlight shined.

Sam recognized that type of metal cup. It belonged inside a lunchbox that crew members brought to the set. They packed their lunches; Sam wouldn't pay to cater the hired help's food, even on 16-hour days.

Sam lost all doubts about who wore the party costumes. Disgruntled and underpaid crew members found a way to grieve without union representation.

Sam screamed when a hammer thrown from far above hit him on the leg, dropping the executive back to one knee.

"Perfect! Take a knee in contrition, good man!" Creighton yelled. "Now, tilt your head, raise your arm, and reach out!"

Creighton looked at Anna, who remained ever silent but never missed a note playing the organ with one hand. Creighton smiled at her, but she gazed back with a stoic, almost catatonic expression. Creighton smiled to reassure her, thinking such a stressful situation was a bit much for someone so young.

Creighton's attention returned to Sam. The executive kept his one-knee position, but the head tilting and arm reaching proved absent.

"Reach, my brother! Reach!" Creighton's voice echoed through the mansion's basement.

Was basement the right word for this place?

Such disconnected thoughts ran through Sam's head. So much overwhelmed him since Sam no longer stood or sat in a controlled environment. The executive never kneeled in any outside of church and certain disreputable establishments he and other Hollywood bigshots liked visiting.

"Reach, Sam! Reach your hands to God! Ask for forgiveness!" Creighton bellowed. The words registered with Sam, who realized Creighton ceased being himself. The actor swallowed the role and brought the Menace of the Mansion to life. Creighton had a way of getting into a character and becoming the character.

Now was not the time to pontificate about a quirky (read: insane) actor. Sam kept his kneeling position, which added to the drama. The executive had another reason for choosing not to stand. He took enough hits from the partygoers above that he may fall if he tried to stand. Sam didn't need to stand to do what Creighton requested of him. Sam tilted his head back and reached his arm out to a hopefully forgiving God.

Sam paused briefly, mimicking Creighton's style of milking melodramatic performances to evoke a powerful reaction from the audience. A robust response Sam received. A brick hit him right between the shoulder blades, pancake-flattening him face-first to the ground.

"Oh, Sam," Creighton spoke with an admonishment.

The executive remained flat down on the ground, terrified to rise.

"Your audience, Sam," Creighton intoned, "They know fake when they see it."

Debris continued to hit Sam as he tried to follow Creighton's cryptic command to "emote." Sam had years of experience keeping a poker face, and the experience translated to his current situation. Sam pulled deep inside to keep his composure and follow Creighton's command.

Command.

The idea enraged Sam, but he had to perform as told. He'd seen three cold-blooded examples of where Creighton's mind resided.

"Come now, Sam," Creighton chided, "You can do better!"

Sam raised his hand awkwardly and in a stilted way. Following Creighton's direction did little to convey the desired emotional response of contrition - not that Sam didn't already feel very sorry for the disaster on ***The Menace of the Mansion***.

"Oh, no! Do it again!" Creighton appeared dejected that his new star could perform the simple artistic task presented to him. Sam never bothered to learn what his underlings had to endure to achieve success.

Debris pelted Sam as he tried to put his head, arm, hand, and heart into Creighton's preference for genuine repentance. The debris bounced off Sam, humiliating him instead of hurting him. Sam understood full well that's what Creighton wanted more than anything, at least up to now.

One large piece of wall plaster hit Sam in the back of the head. The plaster broke into a hundred pieces and flew over the impromptu set. Luckily, it was only plaster. The impact caused Sam much pain, and he struggled to keep his composure.

Try again, Sam did. Creighton's chiding to "Get on with it!" showed the silent actor turned director seemed short on patience with any more "takes" in front of an invisible camera.

Sam pulled himself back up to one knee, mumbling, "I'm trying, damn it." Sam worried Creighton would hear his mumbling and goad the partygoers to retaliate. The partygoers needed no prompting to retaliate. They continued to rain debris down on Sam, throwing sticks and stones, plaster, wood, lightbulbs, tools, and whatever they had available.

Pain. Sam felt pain run through his body as the small objects continued to hit him. For the first time in years, Sam appreciated the hard work of others while feeling dejection from not controlling the room.

That drove an angry response.

Sam ignored the pain and the pelting, rising higher on one knee and screaming at Creighton, "IF YOU COULD DO BETTER, DO IT YOUR DAMN SELF!"

The organ music ceased, silence filled the room, and the pelting stopped. The partygoers kept still, wondering how Creighton would react to the insult. The host responded with a prolonged laugh that ended when the madman made a point.

"Sam, if I couldn't do better, I wouldn't own this mansion, and you wouldn't come crawling here to ask me to save your company." Creighton paused briefly before noting, "Saving your company means me saving you."

Creighton turned to Anna and said, "The nerve." Anna's quiet expression suggested she wouldn't interfere with Creighton's twisted game. Her internal guilt over Creighton's wife's passing let her defer to Creighton's mad whimsy. She returned to her one-handed organ playing, joining Creighton, who did the same.

"Save him." Creighton couldn't hide his contempt as he spoke the words through gritted teeth. Creighton tilted his head and raised his hand and did so in a better way than Sam ever could. Creighton cheated the scene by not limiting himself to the now-archaic approach of silent film acting and speaking his lines. Creighton directed those lines to the audience above. "Should we save him from the doom in the final scene?"

The partygoers gave their response. They reigned debris on Sam, much debris. It would be hard not to guess how the scene would end.

Creighton wanted a modern-day stoning.

"God damn it, Creighton!" Sam screamed, "I'm sorry!" The word sorry echoed off the wall. The echo reflected the only sound in the mansion's basement besides Creighton and Anna's organ music.

"Show it, Sam, show it," Creighton responded coldly. "Talkie films don't exist here."

Sam bit down to prevent himself from saying anything that would agitate the maniac who devised Sam's impending demise. The executive didn't wish to think he'd meet his end in his old star's basement - at least not this way. A cold shiver ran up Sam's spine. The executive had blocked out any thoughts of dying, thinking he'd outfox Creighton. After all, he had a way of talking Creighton into doing things he didn't want to do back when they made so much money together.

Sam went to raise his hand in the air and tilt his head like Creighton wished. Would Creighton appreciate the effort this time?

Sam struck the requested pose, and time stopped for a second. Then Sam felt a heavy and ironic impact. A metal lunchbox hit him on the side of the head, and Sam collapsed to the ground. He didn't move. Sam wanted to move, but his body failed to respond. The spotlight gave him an indication of why - he looked at the ground and saw blood pooling. The metal lunchbox opened another gash on his head.

"Perfect."

As small rocks landed on him, Sam believed the throwers had legitimate gripes. Sam's contrition proved equally legitimate. Considering he said no words, he kept his remorse to himself.

Debris began to fall on Sam. Pieces of wood, plaster, bricks, tools - whatever the partygoers got their hands on, they threw down on the guest of honor. Large pieces missed him, but a fading Sam knew he wouldn't maintain such luck.

"So real. So real." Creighton directed the words to Anna, saying, "The contrition. It's real."

"How do you know?"

Anna finally spoke, never missing a note with her one-handed organ playing.

Creighton missed his note when he ceased finger tapping when the usually silent girl's question caught him by surprise. Creighton smiled when he turned to answer.

Creighton raised an eyebrow in ham-actor fashion, tilting his head in the question's direction. "Dear girl, I was a silent movie star. I know body language. Some things you can't fake."

More debris rained down on Sam. The executive tried to crawl off the platform, but heavier and more damage-inducing debris continued to hit him.

"I thought you said he lies a lot."

Unlike the barely conscious Sam, Creighton didn't feel stunned that Anna spoke. Creighton and Anna speak to one another often. Like Creighton, Anna had little to say to Sam or any other Hollywood monster.

Not that Creighton didn't wonder about Anna's curiosity.

"Anna," Creighton replied, "I said he lies often because I can tell when he's lying. He's not saying anything untruthful right now. I can look at him and see into his rotten, miserable, soulless body."

Anna's conversational skills led the partygoers to cease mimicking the mansion set's collapse. They chose to cease out of caution until Creighton and Anna's conversation ended.

"You said you wanted him to feel sorry for what he did. If he's sorry, why don't you tell them to stop throwing things?" Anna's question forced the talkative Creighton to go silent. After a dramatic lull, Creighton gave his response.

"I say a lot of things, Anna."

"You said he told you your wife wasn't right for the part." When Anna made that comment, Creighton stopped playing the organ. No words came from his mouth. The silent actor went silent.

"Was he lying then? Is that why you made him cast your wife?"

"Quiet little Anna, you're not so quiet anymore."

Creighton let the words hang with implications.

Anna took a breath before looking at Sam's futile attempts to crawl off the platform as doom-inducing debris landed on him. She kept staring at the humbled executive as he let out a cry as a much larger piece of rock hit him on the small of his back — perfect aim, thrown to keep him from moving.

"Why are the rocks and things so small?" Anna asked an odd but good question. "Do you want to keep punishing him?"

"Your sympathies, while kind, are misguided."

"He said he's sorry. You wanted him to say he's sorry."

"I wanted him to show contrition. But, yes, sorry is another word for it, albeit less dramatic." Creighton never could let go of his early theater days.

Anna stared at the prone Sam, who curled into a fetal position, remaining only conscious because nothing heavy landed on his head.

"You want him to suffer?" Anna looked directly at Creighton when asking her second question.

"Did you want your aunt to die?" Creighton retorted questions faster than Anna. "Did you want my wife to die? My wife. Your aunt."

Anna went quiet again, kowtowing to her uncle, knowing her place. Sam - like all the others involved in the movie - never knew the relationship. Creighton and Anna kept silent about that fact.

Sam was neither silent or quiet. Anna could make out words coming from his lips. "Help me." Smaller rocks and debris continued to rain on him intermittently. Creighton wanted to drag this out.

Creighton could read the look on Anna's face, prompting him to say, "Do you think any of them cared about the set collapsing on everyone?"

"He's suffering."

"Anna," Creighton tried not to snap at his niece, but snap he did. "Don't you think your aunt and the people working on that film suffered when they were buried under all that plaster, wood, rocks, and who knows what else? Do you think that fat bastard or any of his ilk cared? Do you think any of them felt sorry?"

"The other three didn't feel sorry. He feels sorry."

"He feels sorry he's going to die."

"He's still sorry. Robert wasn't. Mayra wasn't. Conrad? I don't know if he was sorry. He never had a chance to feel sorry, working so hard to get his mask off. Robert and Mayra struggled, too. Did they have a real chance to feel sorry? You said you'd give them a chance."

"You want to see sorry?" Creighton asked. "I'm sorry. No one's more sorry than me." Creighton's simple words sincerely did not convey his emotion about everything. "If I wasn't so sorry and tortured, do you think I'd go through all this trouble?"

"Are you sorry you made him cast Aunt Hilda in the film when he didn't want to?"

"Anna, my little Anna, sorrow is all I know."

"Will this make it better?"

"No."

"So, why?" Anna hoped she could stall to see if her uncle could have a change of heart.

"Why do they put murderers in the electric chair? Or hang them? Or behead them?" Creighton asked the question as the throwing of the debris ceased. The masked partygoers above waited for directions from their leader, a leader who added, "Or stone them?"

Creighton looked up at his entourage and raised his hands in the air like an orchestra conductor. He paused a second and swung his hands downward with tremendous dramatic force. Creighton needed no words since he mimicked the style of his great silent performances.

Bricks and large rocks poured down. Some missed Sam; some did not. The misses represented legitimate errors. The finale arrived. All thrown objects were meant to put an end to Sam and Creighton's guilt.

Anna looked at the bruised and open lacerations on Sam's face. He wouldn't survive the torment much longer, leading Anna to scream, "It's murder!"

Creighton wouldn't even look in her direction. So she ran in front of his gaze, a gaze focused on seeing Sam get what he long deserved.

Anna did more than scream. She rushed to the platform, throwing herself on top of Sam. Bricks and rocks pelted her as she turned and looked at Creighton and hissed, "You'll be a murderer!"

The bricks and rocks kept falling, and one hit Anna, opening a cut. Blood poured down her face and dripped from her chin. Her blood mixed with the blood that now soaked Sam's clothes.

"STOP!" Creighton screamed. "Stop, you imbeciles!"

Creighton ran to the platform, and the partygoer ceased throwing things once he rushed the stage. They knew Creighton never planned a murder-suicide scenario.

"Anna, what are you doing?"

Anna replied to the question with a question. "Why do you keep doing this?"

'Twas a good thing Creighton's stardom came from silent movies, for he had no answer. His facial expressions - oh, they were fantastic! So perfect for a silent movie! The many emotions - conflicted emotions - they conveyed!

In a close-up, audiences would see every nuisance in Creighton's face. What they would not get is a definitive answer to a simple question.

Creighton looked down at the battered and bleeding Sam. Would he survive?

When Creighton left the theater for the more lucrative world of silent movies, he thought he'd taken a tremendous step down as an artist. Today, he finally appreciated the art of saying nothing, for he had no reply.

Cut-Ups

"You brought the wrong bag." Reggie rolled the words with a defeatist tone. Ralphie looked at Reggie with the same blank expression he always gives him and everybody else.

"What's wrong?" Ralphie always asked people, "What's wrong?" when he did something wrong. Or stupid.

"The wrong bag, man, the wrong bag. You grabbed the wrong bag." Reggie held up the bag and shook it.

"What's wrong with it?" Ralphie asked.

"The bag?" Reggie shot back. "Nothing. The bag's okay. I like the bag. It's what's inside it that brings me woe."

Ralphie shot him another blank look. Reggie realized he needed to present his compatriot with a visual aid. He reached into the bag, pulled out a handheld blender, and asked, "What am I going to do with this?"

"Bake a cake." Ralphie laughed at his little joke.

"You wouldn't bake a cake with a handheld or non-portable blender. You need an oven to bake the cake. The blender mixes everything as a prerequisite. Even so, we're not baking any cakes." Reggie pointed in the direction of a body on the floor covered in blood and said, "WE'RE CUTTING UP AND GETTING RID OF A BODY!"

"Not with a handheld blender," Ralphie added.

"No! Not unless we blend the six-foot-three, 200lbs goof into mush and bake a cake with him!" Reggie almost reached the point where he had enough with Ralphie.

Ralphie tried to save face and the original plan, saying, "Let me look in the bag."

"You want to look in the bag? You don't need to look in the bag. I'll tell you what's in the bag. You brought the bag with the kitchen and cooking stuff in it and left the one with the power tools!"

"Let me see."

"Okay, you want to see?" Reggie tried to keep his cool as he reached into the bag and pulled out a soup ladle. "Here. See this? It's all cooking stuff. You didn't grab the power tools bag!"

"You sure?"

"I'm at soup ladle levels of sure!" Reggie's patience almost ran out.

"There's got to be something in the bag we can use. Isn't there a butcher knife or a meat cleaver?"

"Oh, let me see, let me see." Reggie worked his hands around the interior of the bag. "We got egg beaters, and no, like the blender, we can't beat the stiff into a liquid."

"That's a shame since we have the ladle. We could scoop all the red liquid and flush it." Once Ralphie saved enough money from the corpse dismemberment and disposal business, off to a new career in stand-up comedy, he'd go.

"You know what we got? You know what we got that's closest to butcher knives and meat cleavers?"

"No."

"Butter knives."

"You got two butter knives?"

"I got three butter knives."

"We only need two."

"For what?"

"To cut this stiff up."

"You know how long it will take to cut up a stiff with butter knives?"

"Give me two butter knives. I'll use both hands."

Reggie took a turn at giving his partner a blank stare. The blank stare stepped aside, deferring to a yapping jaw and an accompanying snarky comment. "Sure. Why not? Where have I got to go in the next 12 hours?"

"Where do you got to go?"

Reggie had no comeback to the question because he had nowhere to go.

Ralphie took the initiative by taking a butter knife out of the bag and walking over to the corpse.

"How'd you get good at cutting up and getting rid of bodies?" Ralphie queried.

"Practice." Reggie gave an honest response.

"Think positive about all the time it's going to take to cut up this body," Ralphie said as he kneeled by the corpse. "You're at the point where you can cut a body up on autopilot. So, you go slower when using a butter knife. Big deal. Why not use the time to get good at something else? Why let your head suffer by complaining? Put your hands to work on one thing and your head to work on something else."

Ralphie grabbed the corpse's left hand and started cutting away with the butter knife. The dull blade sliced through the skin better than expected, although cutting muscle proved tougher. Cutting through bone would be even tougher. Ralphie didn't want to think about the job's difficulty level, so he asked his pal a question to divert his mind. "Is there something you wish you were better at?"

"Singing opera."

"No. Seriously."

"Singing opera." The same words, but they came out more emphatic the second time around.

"So sing."

Reggie kneeled on the other side of the corpse, grabbed its right hand, and started cutting with the butter knife. Reggie knew the job would be challenging and the night long. While the stiff lay long dead, time needed killing.

The sound of someone singing opera poorly soon filled the room. Three hours later, the singing improved sharply.

About the Author

Anthony M. Caro is a full-time writer who penned *Tragedy Man: A Horror Anthology*, the essay collection *Universal Monsters & Neurotics: Children of the Night and Their Hang-Ups*, and the sci-fi novelette *Why is Cal Drawing Stick Figures at 3 AM in the 22nd Century?* He has contributed essays and articles to online and print publications, including *Horror News*, *Comic Book Historians*, *Cinema Scholars*, *The Jiu-Jitsu Times*, and *PopMatters*. He's worked in radio, TV, film, and theater.